DEAD FOR GOOD

DEAD FOR GOOD

DEAD FOR GOOD

Dead For Good Book One

STACY CLAFLIN

NOLON KING

STERLING & STONE

Chapter One

BRADLEY MORRIS LOWERED his baseball cap and sipped from his empty coffee cup, waiting. Watching.

His target was due to walk through the door any moment.

The door remained closed.

Conversations from other customers distracted him. One lady at the next table over laughed like a hyena. It grated on his nerves.

He'd rather wait for his target out in the parking lot. Quieter locations were always preferred. But Bradley worked with what he had.

This target literally worked in a Target.

The irony wasn't lost on him.

Juan Sanchez had been making coffee beverages for the last hour. Should've only been only ten minutes after Brad arrived, but he had agreed to cover for a barista who was running late.

It was like he knew his life was on the line.

He should've thought of that before torturing those kids.

He'd evaded the police, so now he was Brad's assignment.

That meant he wouldn't see tomorrow, and the world would be a safer place in a few short hours.

The door marked "Employees" opened.

Brad glanced over, careful not to move his head.

Bingo.

It was Juan.

But he didn't head for the exit as expected. No, he marched deeper into the store.

Brad held back an eye roll as he crumpled his cup and tossed it into a bin, keeping watch on his man.

Juan marched toward the lingerie department, where he began flirting with the girl behind the counter. She had to be half his age.

Brad stopped across the aisle and pretended to be interested in a shirt with the band logo for Goths in Trees as he eyed the creep from across the aisle.

The girl on the other side of the counter inched away from him, her gaze darting around. Juan moved closer, his voice growing louder and his posture stiffening. The girl stepped away from the counter and pushed a cart full of merchandise, keeping it between her and him.

Smart girl.

She kind of reminded him of Hadley, whose performance he was missing because of his job. His seventeen-year-old was the star of her school play, and he wasn't there to cheer her on from the front row.

Because of Juan.

But he was making the world a better place for Hadley. For his whole family.

The girl across the aisle backed away from Juan, her eyes growing wider by the moment. A wall display of lacy robes cornered her.

Juan inched around the cart.

She shook her head and held out her palms.

He laughed.

Brad shoved the shirt back on the rack. It was too soon for his target to see him, but Brad couldn't let this continue. He grabbed a strappy, pleated thing and hurried over. "Excuse me, miss. I believe this is the right size for my wife. Can you ring this up for me?"

Juan glowered at Brad, his face contorting and reddening.

"I appreciate all your help finding this." Brad slapped the lingerie onto the counter. Glared back at Juan.

The girl threw him an appreciative glance.

He turned back to Juan. "I'm not interrupting you, am I?"

Juan's expression said it all.

Brad stared him down until he trudged away.

"Thank you so much." The girl breathed a sigh of relief. "I was really getting scared. Are you actually buying that?"

"No." Brad watched Juan hurrying away. "I gotta go."

"Thanks again!"

Brad gave a quick wave and followed Juan, hurrying not to lose him.

This time, his target went for the exit.

He stopped briefly to pocket some gum, giving Brad enough time to catch up.

He kept enough distance to avoid the other man's attention.

Once outside, Juan darted to the left toward the side of the building.

Brad sprinted toward Juan.

Fingers squeezed his arm. Then his other arm. Something covered his eyes. His mouth. Shoved him against the brick wall. Pain shot through his cheek.

His mind raced to make sense of it. Nothing like this had ever happened during a hit. He was always overly cautious.

Brad kicked his assailants. Elbowed them. Thrashed around. Flung himself like he'd been trained.

One of the men flew back, let go of Brad's eyes.

Juan was running across the lot. Still in sight.

For now.

The other attacker grasped him harder, swearing profusely.

Brad punched him as hard as he could in the face.

His assailant blocked instinctively.

Brad kicked his knee.

He fell to the pavement with a thud. Reached up. Hollered in pain.

The other man flew into Brad's side. They crashed against the wall. Landed on the other attacker.

Brad shoved him off. Leaped to his feet. Glanced around.

Juan was nearing the edge of the parking lot. Whether he got into a car or left on foot, it would be next to impossible to catch him if he didn't go now.

He would have to start over. Admit defeat to his boss.

That wasn't going to happen.

His two attackers leaped up. Lunged for him.

Brad backed up, reached into his inside jacket pocket, and yanked out the bear spray he kept for emergencies.

They screamed — blinded by a sudden and unexpected agony.

He raced toward Juan, no longer having the luxury of trying to stay quiet or out of sight. His shoes thudded on the concrete.

Juan turned toward a dark van.

The man wasn't going to get away. Not on his watch.

Brad forced his legs to run faster. His muscles burned, his lungs on fire.

It wasn't until Juan was almost within reach that he turned toward Brad. "What the—"

Brad aimed the bear spray and pressed the nozzle.

It wasn't his typical MO. But it did the job.

Brad grabbed the man by his throat. "You're coming with me."

Chapter Two

BRAD LOWERED the visor and turned on the harsh overhead light to check for bruising in the mirror. Only a slight purpling near his right temple. Faye probably wouldn't notice.

He grabbed the plastic container with the two desserts from La Isla's, her favorite restaurant near the Space Needle. They hadn't been there since before Luna was born. Seven years. He grimaced at the realization, then winced at the sore spot near his eye.

Stepping outside into the frigid drizzle, something pinched in his lower back. He rubbed the spot as he balanced the cheesecake and set the alarm for his black Mercedes. A dull ache radiated from his knee as he made his way to the front door. Maybe he should start considering retirement.

No. He was one of the best assassins at BlueBlade. His only real competition was Rose Flores, and that was because he'd been the one to train her — a rarity, as most who joined the company already knew what they were doing. He only had aches and pains tonight was because he'd been jumped. He'd be fine otherwise.

Brad entered the house and kicked off his shoes. The soft thud as they bumped into his daughter's cleats sounded louder in the late-night silence. He cringed, half-expecting Faye to appear at the top of the stairs to scold him for making so much noise while the kids slept. Except they were probably still awake — at least the older two, Hadley and Zeke.

He crept up the stairs, not wanting to wake Luna. The master bedroom was as dim as the hallway, and he almost didn't see Faye lying in bed.

"Are you awake?" He gave her a peck on the cheek, brushing against something cold. "Why the ice pack?" He imagined her with bruising, too.

Faye moaned. "Migraine."

"Oh, no. I thought you were past those."

"They still hit me from time to time." Her tone indicated that this wasn't exactly news.

"Can I get you anything?" He rubbed her shoulder.

She pulled away. "I just need sleep."

"I picked up chocolate caramel cheesecake slices from La Isla's." He held out the box.

"Not so loud."

Brad stiffened. "I'll put it in the fridge. We can share it tomorrow."

"Or the kids can have it."

"I got it for you."

"I don't need the extra calories."

"You look perfect. No need to change anything."

"Goodnight." Faye rolled away from him.

"Sorry I didn't call about being late. Figured you'd already be sleeping."

Silence.

"I'll put this in the fridge." He changed into a T-shirt and sweats, then headed back downstairs.

Hadley sat at the table tapping furiously on her phone, her hair in a bun and her face slathered with green goo. "Another late night at the office?"

Brad opened the fridge. "Just got back from a convention."

"How exciting."

"You have no idea." He moved some food around in the fridge until the cheesecake fit.

She pulled her attention from the screen and met his gaze. "You coming to my play tomorrow? The evening show is the final performance."

"I wouldn't miss it."

Her eyebrows furrowed. "I'm the lead. You haven't made it to any yet."

"Of *this* play, and I'll be there. My calendar is cleared for it."

"If you say so." Hadley turned back to her phone.

"I will. Tomorrow night. What time?"

"Seven-thirty." She left the room.

Brad rubbed his temples, tempted to eat the cheese-cake. Instead, he grabbed a beer and went into the back-yard. The drizzle had turned into rain mixed with snow. Ignoring the goosebumps forming along his arms, he collapsed onto the bench swing and took a long swig. The drink did nothing to calm his nerves.

After emptying the bottle, he rose, eager to get back to the warmth inside. But then he paused while reaching for the handle. The house next door was completely dark. His neighbor usually left several lights on all night. It was one of the many things about Duke that annoyed him.

Brad shook it off and returned to the kitchen. He poured some ice into a large glass in case Faye wanted more for her pack. On the way to his room, he checked on his son.

Zeke had on his gaming headphones and sat in front of his computer, unaware Brad had opened the door. He checked on his youngest next, fully expecting to find Luna sound asleep.

She was sitting by her door in the dark, petting the ragdoll cat, Mittens.

"What are you doing up?"

Luna shrugged.

"It's late for little girls." Brad pulled her into his arms and settled her into her bed. Mittens scampered away. "Were you waiting for me to get home?"

"Maybe."

"I'm here. Time to get some sleep." He tucked her in and kissed her forehead.

"Okay."

Brad waited until she closed her eyes before heading to his room and climbing into bed with Faye. "Do you need more ice?"

"You don't need to go back down."

"I brought some up."

"You did?" She sat up.

"Yes." He took the pack and tried to put ice in it but dropped the cubes on their bed. "I need to turn on the light."

She squinted as the room when bright. "You didn't need to bring that up."

"I wanted to."

The corners of her mouth curved up slightly.

Warmth spread through his chest. He handed her the refilled ice pack.

She leaned closer as if to give him a kiss but then paused, her mouth gaping.

Probably noticed his bruise.

"Is that blood behind your ear?"

His heart plummeted. How had he missed that? He straightened his sore back. "It's nothing. A guy cut himself at the convention. Some people shouldn't be allowed near knife shows."

"You helped clean him up?"

"Right." He rubbed the spot behind his ear, feeling a small crusty patch, and turned off the light. "Looks like I should shower off."

"Probably. Thanks for the ice."

Brad sauntered to the bathroom, hardly able to believe he'd made such a rookie mistake. Sure, things hadn't gone as planned, but he needed to stay at the top of his game.

From here on out, he would make sure he did.

No excuses.

Chapter Three

BRAD KISSED Faye and then sat at the kitchen table, his stomach grumbling from the aroma of bacon and waffles. He'd have offered to help, but she loved making her Saturday morning spread, and he knew better than to get in her way.

It was late enough that both his teens were awake and eating. Hadley had even dressed and curled her hair.

"Good morning." He forced a smile, still half-asleep, and sipped his coffee.

"Morning," Zeke mumbled.

Hadley nodded but didn't look up from her phone.

"Mom got chocolate syrup." Luna beamed petting Mittens.

"That's great." Brad set his mug down. "No pets at the table."

Luna pouted.

He shook his head. "You know the rules."

Zeke snickered.

"What?" Brad inhaled more caffeine.

"Nothing. Hey, Dad, did you know Michael Dukakis

11

declared April 24th 'New Kids On the Block Day' in Massachusetts?"

"I must've missed that one."

"And the first emoticon was used in 1982." Zeke grinned.

A dramatic sigh from Hadley, then, "Would you stop already?"

Luna nudged the cat, who jumped to the floor, then leaned closer to Brad. "Mom lets me hold her at mealtime when you're away."

"You still know the rules."

Faye came over and piled more waffles onto the plate in the middle of the table. She rubbed Brad's shoulders. "You feel tense."

He closed his eyes for a moment. "That feels nice. Is your headache gone?"

"Just needed to sleep it off. Luckily it wasn't the kind that lasts for days." She took the seat next to him and grabbed a piece of bacon.

"Then you'd have to cook." Luna poked Brad and giggled.

"Nobody wants that." Hadley looked up from her phone.

"Luna actually pays attention to her family."

She smirked before returning to her screen. Another battle Brad didn't bother to fight.

"All done." Luna leaped from her chair and scampered out of the room.

Faye turned to Brad. "Does she seem off to you?"

"Off?"

"She isn't acting like herself this morning."

"Seems fine to me." He took a bite of waffle.

Zeke glanced between them. "Thanks, Mom. It was great." He raced out of the room.

"Dishes!" Faye called after him.

Hadley pushed back her chair. "Don't look at me. I have to do my makeup for the play and need to be at school in less than an hour."

Faye shook her head. "What happened to the kids who did their chores without hounding?"

"Are you talking about our kids?" One corner of Brad's mouth curved up. "I'll get the dishes this time."

She gave him a double-take. "You will?"

"Don't look so surprised."

"I'm not." She pushed what was left of her waffle around the plate before looking back at him. "I was thinking about the salon again."

"What about it?"

"I was—"

"Cheryl isn't giving you problems about your hours again, is she? That woman needs to understand that you have a family. You want me to talk to her?"

"No. And she isn't bothering me."

"What, then?"

"I want to open my own salon here in the house."

"Not this again." Brad's jaw clenched. "We've been over this. It won't work."

"Why not? The house is big enough, and with all the kids in school all day, it'll work perfectly. I won't have to waste time on my commute and—"

"We don't need people traipsing through the house at all hours of the day."

Her eyes narrowed. "They won't be. I can use that storage room by the entry. It'll be easy to convert. People won't have to go any farther than that. I can even attach the bathroom."

"I don't like it."

"Why not?"

"We've been over this a thousand times."

Faye leaned back and folded her arms. "So, it's all about what you want. Again."

"Are you kidding me? I'm gone so much — what if something happens? I won't be here to do anything."

"I'm not a damsel who needs rescuing. And I have more than enough clients who would follow me. I wouldn't have to lose part of my income to the salon. Do you realize how much of my money goes to Cheryl?"

Brad started to reply, but the doorbell rang. "Crackerjack timing."

"We're not done here."

"I'm sure we're not."

"I've got it!" Luna whizzed through the kitchen.

Brad rose. "I'd better see who that is."

"And I'll do the dishes."

"I told you I'll get them."

"Wouldn't want to put you out."

He drew a deep breath and marched toward the door.

Luna flung it open, and two uniformed officers darkened the doorway.

Brad's stomach knotted. They must have discovered what he did for his line of work. "Can I help you?" he asked, standing beside his daughter.

The woman looked at him with a pinched expression. "I'm Detective Stewart, and this is Officer McKinnon. We need to ask you a few questions."

This was it.

Brad straightened his back. "Right here is fine." He turned to Luna. "You can go to your room, honey."

"But Daddy. I—"

"I said go."

She frowned before trudging up the stairs.

"Police! Cool." Zeke thundered down.

Faye appeared at Brad's side. "What's the matter?"

The woman looked around him. "We have a few questions."

"Come in." Faye waved them to the sitting room.

Brad glared at her, not that she noticed. As long as the cops didn't go any farther, he could keep everything under control.

Everyone settled on the couches. Zeke fidgeted, twisting his wild hair.

The detective made eye contact with each of them before speaking. "Where were you last night between six and eight?"

Brad didn't blink. He'd been killing his target. They couldn't know about that.

"I was playing video games." Zeke grinned. "Why?"

Officer McKinnon scribbled on a tablet.

Brad opened his mouth to tell them about his supposed knife convention, but Faye spoke first.

"Our oldest daughter was performing in her play, and our two youngest were here. Brad and I were together all night. Date night."

The lie knocked the air from his lungs.

The two officers turned to Brad. "Is that what happened?"

Faye turned to Brad, her eyes pleading with him to agree with her story.

"Sir?" said Detective Stewart.

Brad turned to her. "Yes, we were together last night."

"Where? Doing what?"

He turned to Faye. "Maybe you should tell them."

"We went to a movie and had dinner," she said.

Two things they would never be able to prove. He should've come up with something faster.

"What's going on?" Brad asked. "Why do you need to know where we were?"

The detective studied him. "There was a murder last night."

"Murder?" Faye exclaimed. "Where?"

"Next door. I'm sorry to inform you that Duke Hill died last night."

Brad heard a gasp, then turned to see Hadley in the doorway, her mouth gaping. She ran up the stairs.

"He's dead?" Zeke stared into space.

"Duke?" A mixture of shock and relief washed through Brad. They knew nothing of his assassinations, but his neighbor had been murdered.

The two officers traded a look, and the man made more notes. The woman leaned forward, her attention on Brad. "Tell us about your relationship with the deceased."

He cleared his throat. "Nothing unusual."

"No?" the detective asked. "Some people say you two had a feud."

"Feud?" Brad laughed.

Faye glared at him.

"We had friendly competitions. Nothing more."

"Tell me about those."

Brad shrugged. "It's our thing. Everyone knows we vie to have the best-decorated house at Christmastime or the best fireworks on the Fourth."

"Fireworks are illegal, Dad!" Zeke shook his head.

The detective turned to Zeke. "We're not here to issue citations for fireworks."

"That does explain the decorations outside," said Officer McKinnon.

Brad nodded. "Exactly. Duke is — *was* — rooting for the Steelers to win the Super Bowl tomorrow."

"And you're rooting for the Panthers."

"Just a friendly competition." Brad put his arm around Faye and gave the officers a reassuring smile. "In fact, Duke invited us to his place for his Super Bowl party tomorrow. If we hated each other, do you think he'd do that?"

The officers exchanged another glance. They knew something. Probably that Faye was lying, and he was covering for her.

"Did you see anything unusual last night?"

"We were *out*. Remember?" Brad nodded.

"Right. We'll need the names of the restaurant and theater."

Brad turned to his wife.

"Yeah, sure. Let me get my purse." Faye stood and hurried out of the room.

The man turned to Brad. "What do you do for a living?"

"Sell knives."

"You do?"

"Yes." He studied them, trying to determine their angle.

"What company?"

They were asking too many questions. He glanced around the corner for Faye but didn't see her. "BlueBlade."

Another traded glance, this one with widening eyes. The detective turned to him. "Tell us more about that."

Brad leaned back. "Not much to tell. I'm a salesman."

"How long have you worked there?"

"Since 2008. After the economy crashed, so did my thriving real estate business."

"You've been with them since then?"

"Yes." Brad tried to keep the edge out of his voice.

"So, you'd say you know BlueBlade knives well?"

"I'm one of their top employees. Why? Was he killed with one?"

Now it looked like the officers were trying *not* to look at one another.

He had been. The dead neighbor who Brad openly didn't like had been slaughtered with one of his company's knives.

And Brad was lying about his whereabouts when the murder occurred.

Couldn't come clean, and not just because he'd been killing Juan Sanchez at the same time — he had to cover for his wife's deception as well.

He needed to find out why she was lying.

Chapter Four

FAYE PRESSED her palm against the wall as Brad let the police out, trying to ignore her pounding heart. She should've just said that she'd been home with a migraine. Like she had told Brad.

Now he knew she'd been lying. At least he'd gone with it. And his elaborate descriptions of the knives he worked with had distracted the officers enough to at least temporarily forget about the details of their nonexistent movie and dinner.

But they'd be back. They would want details. At least, that would give her time to think of something believable. She never should've said they were out places where people could say they had or hadn't seen them. She was a terrible liar.

Brad closed the door and turned to her, his expression tight.

Her stomach lurched, and her body went cold.

"What was that about?" His gaze bored into hers.

She swallowed, her thoughts racing. "I can't believe

there was a murder next door! Just a few feet away from our house. Next to where the kids and I—"

"Don't say that too loudly," he said, stepping closer.

"What?"

"That *you* were here."

"I … I don't know why I told them we were out together."

"You don't *know* why?" He leaned in, barely leaving any space between them. "What was wrong with telling them you had a headache?"

She tried to back up but bumped into the wall. "It's hardly an alibi. Here with a kid who was glued to his computer the whole time and a seven-year-old."

"I sure wasn't here. You brought me into this lie. Now, what are we going to do?"

Tears threatened. "It was the only thing I could think of!"

"Those cops will be back. They're going to want more information on our 'date' last night. Where did we go?"

"I'll come up with something. At least we know it wasn't a sushi restaurant."

"Huh?"

"I've been trying to get you to try sushi for years."

"Yeah, and I'll never eat it. But we don't need to figure out where we *didn't* eat. Like La Isla's."

"No. That's too far. And they only sell desserts."

"If you remember, I *did* go there last night. Remember the cheesecake?"

"I know. But you were there alone. That doesn't work. And besides, I said I'll figure it out. But first, I need another ice pack."

"You're going to lie down now?"

"I need to think." She raced to the kitchen and refilled her ice pack.

"What are you hiding?"

She licked her lips and squeezed her eyes shut. No way she could tell her husband that she might've been the last person to see Duke before his death.

"Faye?"

She spun around. "I really do have a headache. It was better, but now it's a hundred times worse. Give me a few minutes."

"We need to talk about this now."

"I said, give me some time!" Pressure squeezed her temples as she raced up the stairs, nearly knocking over Luna. "Sorry, sweetie."

She closed the bedroom door and threw herself on the bed, gasping for air. Trying to make sense of the last hour. Waging a war with her tears.

Duke was dead, killed in cold blood, just one house away from her family. How could that be? Dead. Barely an hour after she'd cut his hair in their kitchen.

Brad would be furious on so many levels. For one, he hadn't liked the guy — got upset whenever she or the kids spoke with him. Hated the fact that the twenty-something was always trying to show him up. But Duke always came into the salon asking specifically for her. What was she supposed to do? Say no? Because her husband didn't like it? Everyone would think she was a submissive mouse.

She'd been cutting his hair and chatting with him for at least a year now. But last night had been his first time in her home. He'd come over, begging for a quick trim. Needed it right away and offered twice the usual fee. And she didn't even have to give any to the salon. It was all hers.

She'd loved every moment of it, as much as Brad would seethe if he knew. Faye had imagined her home salon the entire time she worked on his hair. The only reason she couldn't was because her husband was so obsessed with his privacy. As if she'd let her clients go through the house.

Brad didn't trust her.

The door burst open, and Brad's footsteps thundered toward the bed. "We need to discuss this now. The neighbors are gathered next door, and the police are talking to as many as they can."

She readjusted the ice pack over her eyes.

"This isn't going away! They'll be back. Maybe in minutes. The way that detective was eyeing us — there's no way she's buying our story. We need to figure out the details *now*."

She sat up and glared at him. "We didn't kill him. What are you so worried about?"

Brad paced. "We just lied to the cops about a murder."

"No. About our alibis. Big difference. We didn't commit a murder."

He jolted to a stop. "If they find out we lied, they'll assume that we did."

She relaxed a little. At least he wasn't asking about why she lied ... yet. "Dinner and a movie."

"Where? What time? Who saw us? Did you think about that?"

Her mind went blank. "We, uh, ordered in."

"You said we weren't here."

"We ate at a hotel."

"Got a receipt?" He cocked a brow.

"No, because we paid cash."

"What hotel? Can we convince a receptionist to vouch for seeing us?"

Tears blurred her vision. "I'm sorry, I shouldn't have said anything."

Brad wrapped an arm around her. "We'll figure something out. What about your parents' cabin? It's close enough to use for an evening to get away from the kids."

She wiped her eyes. "That might work — if we don't word it like that. If nobody else was there at the time."

"Any way to find out?"

"I can call Mom."

"Do that. I'm going to look outside again and see what's going on next door."

Faye laced her fingers through his and looked into his eyes. "Thank you for not being mad at me."

"We're in this together. Always and forever." He pressed his lips to her forehead.

She hated lying to him.

Chapter Five

THE CROWD OUTSIDE HAD GROWN. Brad grabbed a coat and slid it on before heading outside to find out what people were saying. Did anyone think he would actually kill the neighbor? Sure, he'd never been a fan of the guy — not by a long shot — but that didn't mean he wanted him dead. Duke had been young and arrogant but likely would've outgrown that with time. Especially if he ever got married.

Brad zipped his jacket all the way up as the chilly air hit him. His breath formed a puff of smoke. Just as he was closing the door, someone tugged it open.

Hadley stood there in too much makeup — for the production he'd promised to attend that day — and red eyes. She'd been crying. Over the fool next door? It shouldn't surprise him. She and Faye often sobbed over puppy commercials and romcoms.

"You okay, kiddo?"

She nodded. "Gotta go. I'm running late."

"Need anything?"

"Nope." She darted past him and into her car, parked

down the street. Otherwise, she wouldn't have been able to get around the curious neighbors.

He closed the door and made his way to the sidewalk. The property was blocked off with yellow caution tape, with uniforms swarming in and out of the house alongside plainclothes detectives. A Steelers flag hung proudly by the door — larger than the Panthers flag Brad had put up on his own porch.

A hand rested on his arm. "Can you believe he's dead?"

Brad turned toward Lisa from down the street. "It's horrifying."

"I just can't imagine someone murdering Duke. There's never been a nicer guy. He fixed my toilet when Cory was out of town." She wiped her eyes and turned back to Duke's house.

He perked his ears to a whispered conversation right next to him.

"Who would do this?"

"And to Duke, of all people?"

He clenched his jaw. Had nobody else seen their neighbor for who he really was? Or was the man being immortalized in the aftermath of his murder? People tended to only focus on the good in the deceased as if death automatically diluted the truth. Even his own family was upset, and they hardly knew the guy.

Sure, it was rattling to have a murder so close to home, but it wasn't *that* shocking for Duke to be the target. The guy had practically been asking for it, the way he always had to be number one: best neighbor, best handyman, best cook, best everything. He had probably exhibited the same basic behavior in every other part of his life.

Brad knew better than to verbalize any of that. Most people didn't even consider any of this, mourning only the idealized version of the departed. It was human nature. Brad had once been there. Until his own father's murder. Then he'd learned to see people realistically. Nobody was ever perfect. Everyone had a good side and a bad side. And you could only see what a person was willing to show you.

He wandered around, offering condolences to his troubled neighbors but mostly listening to conversations. His name hadn't come up. Good. That meant nobody took his ongoing feud with Duke seriously — or at least nobody was voicing it.

But the police had known. Someone had told them.

A hush ran through the crowd as two CSI investigators exited the house with sealed bags. A flurry of whispers surrounded him. He tried to see what they were carrying, but the bags weren't transparent.

Could the murder weapon be in one? He narrowed his eyes, looking for the outline of a knife.

Someone tapped his shoulder. "Looks like the Hatfield has lost his McCoy."

"Excuse me?" Brad whipped around.

"You know what I mean." Lucas from the other side of the street patted a chihuahua with a pink bow on her collar that was nearly as big as her head. The dog shook in his arms.

"Afraid I don't. You should take your dog inside. She looks cold."

"Mitzy's fine." He rubbed the pup's head, then spoke in a high voice. "Bit of a nervous Nelly, aren't you?"

Brad stepped away, but not before Lucas turned back to him.

"You and Duke were always going at it. Look at your houses now. It's like the NHL exploded right here."

"NFL," Brad corrected. "And it's nothing more than a friendly competition. We laughed about it all the time."

"Really?"

"Yes." He turned back to the crime scene.

More CSIs brought out evidence as officers continued going in and out of the house.

Brad weaved his way through the neighbors, listening.

One more person stopped him and brought up the feud between him and Duke.

"The man is *dead*," Brad blurted. "A life taken needlessly, and all anyone can think about is our friendly rivalry. Seriously, what do you people think of me?"

More than a dozen people turned and stared.

"That's right!" he continued. "This is the last thing I wanted — the last thing he deserved. I wasn't even home at the time, so you can all stop pointing fingers and start trying to figure out who actually did this."

Several people spoke, but Brad marched away before saying something he might regret. He and Faye didn't even have a solid alibi yet.

A round of gasps as he reached the edge of the property, then turned back to see the coroners bringing out the body bag.

He paused and took in the sight, a heaviness settling over him as the reality of his dead neighbor washed over him.

As the coroners turned, the side of the bag showed the logo for Winchester body bags. The company had gone under more than a year earlier. That meant the city probably got the bags on clearance.

He chuckled at the thought.

Neighbors turned and glared.

Brad covered his mouth and coughed.

Lucas, still patting the quivering dog, gave him the stink-eye.

The detective made eye contact, then started walking toward him.

Brad hurried inside. He needed to speak with his boss immediately.

Before things got even more out of control.

Chapter Six

FAYE PACED THE HALL, pausing every so often outside Brad's locked office. He was on the phone, but the words were too muffled to make anything out. Was he consulting with an attorney? Talking to his boss? Kurt seemed to know every lawyer in the state of Washington.

She stopped and leaned against the wall, taking deep breaths. Not that it slowed her pounding heart. How could she have lied to the police? The words had spilled out of her mouth before she had time to consider the implications. But at least they wouldn't look at her as the last person to see Duke alive.

Unless the truth came out.

Brad had promised it wouldn't. Things may have been rocky between them recently, but he was a man of his word. They'd been through hell and back over the years, and they would make it through this, too.

Besides, her lie didn't matter. It wasn't like she'd killed the guy. She'd only cut his hair. Right before he was murdered.

Blood drained from her body. What if her prints were

on him? Her mind raced, going over every moment she'd spent with him. Her hands had been busy with the comb and scissors. If she'd touched anything, it'd only been his hair. The police couldn't get prints off that, surely. Besides, he'd run gel through it before leaving. Any traces of her should be gone.

Unless she'd dropped skin cells, or he'd picked up one of her strands of hair.

No, that was crazy. She watched too many crime dramas. This was real life.

Maybe Duke had said something that might offer her a clue as to who would soon kill him. He'd been excited about his girlfriend, it was a big weekend for her, and he'd wanted to look his best. Anything else?

Work. He'd talked about his job, which seemed like a joke, but actually did well for him since he'd been able to buy a house in their neighborhood as a single guy. He was a top seller of fitness products for a multi-level marketing company and made bank selling courses to other MLM hopefuls. But it hadn't come up in their conversation the night before.

Or had it? Faye hadn't been paying particularly close attention. It wasn't like she'd expected him to be dead within hours. She'd been more concerned about Brad coming home early and freaking out about Duke being in their house. He got annoyed when Faye said hi to the guy, so he'd lose it if he saw him in their house.

Brad raised his voice in his office.

She scooted closer to the door and strained to make out any words. It sounded like he said blade, not that it would be surprising if he were talking to Kurt. They both lived and breathed knives, collecting them. Kurt seemed determined to own every expensive luxury blade ever produced, while Brad was drawn to antiques. The reason he'd installed the fancy lock on his office door was to make sure the children would never discover his collection and accidentally hurt themselves.

Her husband's voice softened, and again she tried to recall an important detail of her brief time with Duke the night before. The only thing that stood out was his girl-friend. It seemed unlikely that she could have done it, given how he talked about her. The man had been head-over-heels, his expression lighting up with every word dedicated to her as the subject. If he was to be believed, the woman walked on water. Faye had thought the girlfriend was lucky — his excitement brought back memories of the days Brad had looked at her like that — and she had hoped the lady might soon become her neighbor. Faye could use a friend who wasn't superficial, like so many of her neighbors.

The office door flung open, and Brad stepped into the hall.

She spun around.

"Were you listening to me?"

"No. I was waiting."

The lines around his eyes were deeper now. "Doesn't matter. I don't have anything to hide. What about you?"

She swallowed, forcing away images of Duke in their kitchen. "No."

"Why did you lie to the cops?"

"I told you—"

He stepped closer, his expression softening. "I need the truth. For the cover story to work, I need to know exactly what happened last night."

"It was nothing. I need you to trust me."

"Trust you? You're lying."

"Not to you." Her pulse drummed in her ears.

His mouth formed a straight line, but he put a gentle hand on her arm. "Faye, honey, we're on the same team. I have to come up with a whole new alibi because of something you blurted to the police. Let *me* in."

She swallowed. "In the bedroom."

He threaded his fingers through hers and led her down the hallway. They sat on the bed, the silence seeming to linger forever.

She squeezed his hand. "We're going to get through this, just like everything else over the years. I was Zeke's age when we first got together. Can you believe that? I can't picture him with a girlfriend, but that's how old I was. And you were—"

"I don't need a history lesson. I was there, remember?"

"Yes, but sometimes it helps to think about the things we've accomplished. We've survived so much. Your dad's murder—"

Brad stiffened. "Don't bring that up."

Her breath hitched. "I'm just saying we got through that together. You've always said I was your rock. If we could manage that as teenagers, we can definitely navigate this now that we have teens of our own."

"What does age have to do with anything? Stop trying to change the subject. Why did you lie about last night? Kurt is going to find us an attorney, and we have to tell that attorney the truth — as quickly as possible. Those people charge by the hour. Aside from that, if you can't tell me what really happened, what do we have together?"

His words were like an arrow to the heart. But at the same time, he could see the truth as a betrayal. Especially if he found out that she cut Duke's hair every other week at the salon. Most husbands wouldn't care because it was totally innocent, but not hers. Brad couldn't stand the guy. Didn't want any of them talking to Duke.

"Well?"

She tried to swallow the lump growing in her throat,

but it only grew bigger as she gathered the nerve to tell him. "I spoke with Duke last night."

Brad tilted his head.

She was not going to cry. "He came over and asked me to trim his hair for a date."

"But you said no." It wasn't a question.

"Duke was desperate. He wanted to look his best for his girlfriend — really wanted to impress her. It had nothing to do with me. Nothing happened."

"You let him into our house?"

"Just the kitchen. It was a quick trim."

"Why you?" Brad's voice rose. "Why not Supercuts down the road?"

"Are you serious? He knew I'm a professional stylist, and *nothing* was open at that hour."

"I can't believe you said yes."

"It was just a trim! And it can't hurt to offer a little friendliness to our neighbors."

"To him, it can."

"He's dead now. What does it matter?"

Brad leaped from the bed. "The doorbell camera. His visit will be on there. What if the cops want to see the footage? They'll find out everything."

"They'll also see that *nothing happened*. He left here alive and well, eager to see his girlfriend."

"We have to tell them about her."

"What?" she exclaimed. "I can't let them know he was over here last night."

"You don't have to. Just say he mentioned it another time. What's one more lie?"

She jolted.

"I need to see the footage." He pulled out his phone and opened the app, tapping on his screen.

Faye's stomach knotted. She didn't have anything to

hide, but Brad would flip when he saw her on the screen talking with Duke.

What if one of them had mentioned her being his regular stylist? She hadn't thought about the camera. Did it pick up voices or just video? Her mind was everywhere at once, making it impossible to think straight. They could talk to people at the door through the app, but that didn't mean the video picked up sound.

Brad swore and held out his phone. "Video proof of the dead guy entering our home."

"I *know*."

"Is there a way to delete this?"

She shrugged. "Never tried."

He tapped the screen furiously. "Does this store back-ups?"

"You're the one who picked out the system."

"I can't remember everything." He didn't look up. "Would you look at the app on your phone and see if you can figure it out? Tick-tock."

She went into the settings and looked around, not seeing anything about cloud back-ups.

Ding-dong!

They exchanged wide-eyed glances.

"Dad!" Zeke called. "The police officers are here again!"

Brad vented a string of profanities. "We're leaving the phones up here."

Chapter Seven

BRAD HURRIED DOWN THE STAIRS, stopping only to send Luna to her room.

Thankfully, Zeke hadn't yet opened the door.

Brad put an arm around his son. "Just tell them you didn't know Duke. That's all you have to say. They have no right to harass us. We didn't do anything wrong."

"Okay."

Knock, knock.

Brad stood taller and answered the door. "What a surprise, officers. Can I help you?"

The duo exchanged a look before the detective spoke. "We have a few more questions for you."

He hid his annoyance with a half-smile. "Of course. Ask away."

She glanced behind him. "Can we come in?"

"If it's just a few questions, this should be fine."

"We'd prefer to come in. This won't take long if you cooperate."

"Are you suggesting that I'm not cooperating?"

"Not at all. May we step inside?"

Brad relented but blocked the entrance to the sitting room. "So. Your questions?"

The detective closed the door behind her. "Tell us about your relationship with the deceased."

"We had no relationship — none of us. Barely knew the guy."

Sergeant Lewis arched a brow. "You lived next door to him and had *no* relationship with him?"

"Not much more than a friendly wave every once in a while." Brad looked to Faye and Zeke, who both nodded in agreement.

Detective Stewart took a step closer. "Aside from your feuding?"

"You make it sound like we were enemies. But it was nothing like that. We were friendly competitors, always trying to see who could have the best Christmas decorations or the biggest fireworks show."

"How did that start?" asked Lewis.

Brad drew in a deep breath as he tried to remember. "Everyone always came over here to see the fireworks or holiday decorations. Shortly after Duke moved in, he decided to show the neighborhood what he could do. At some point, it turned into something of a game. I appreciated his efforts, they inspired me. I'd started to get a bit stagnant."

"So, you *enjoyed* the rivalry?" The detective made a note on her tablet.

"Yes. When there's competition, everyone wins. Who loves a monopoly?"

"The person at the top." Lewis stared Brad down.

"Not me. Like I said, Duke was just what I needed. Before he moved in, I had half the Panthers paraphernalia."

The cops exchanged another look before the detective turned to Zeke. "Does that sound right to you?"

"Yeah, totally."

"Did you know Duke?"

Zeke shrugged. "Not really."

"Not *really*?"

"We didn't have anything in common. He is — was — this totally cool dude, and I'm well, me." Zeke pulled on his thick curls and looked down at his shirt, which bore a Dungeons & Dragons reference splattered in what looked like goblin blood across the front.

Brad leaned toward Zeke and tried to get his attention by clearing his throat.

His son didn't look up.

Detective Stewart gave him a funny look and made more notes before turning to Faye. "What about you? Did you know the deceased?"

"Barely knew the guy."

"Never talked to him?"

A beat of silence passed before she answered. "Rarely."

"How often was 'rarely'?" The detective leaned forward.

Brad took advantage of her distraction and waved at Zeke.

Still nothing.

"Every couple of weeks?" Faye said. "I don't know. It wasn't something I paid much attention to."

"And your daughters?" asked Lewis. "How often did they talk to him?"

"They had no interactions with him. None. Not at all."

Brad tensed. She was overdoing it, but he couldn't

expect her to handle these situations as well as he did — she had no experience with any of this.

"None at all?"

"The kids are friendly," Brad interjected. "Surely, they said hello to him. But nothing beyond that. What would they have in common with him to talk about?"

"That's what we're trying to find out."

Brad resisted the urge to clench his fists. "Are you questioning any other neighbors this much?"

"Your name is the one that keeps coming up. Some people seem to think you'd be glad to have him out of the way."

Brad laughed. "Let me guess — bored housewives with nothing better to do than gossip about neighbors?"

She glowered at him. "We'd like to speak with your daughters."

"No. Luna's only seven. She doesn't need to know about any of this."

"And Hadley?"

"Not here." The last thing Brad needed was for them to question his daughter at school.

"Where is she?"

"It doesn't matter because you aren't going to say one word to her without us present. I'm aware of my family's rights."

"Noted. Where is Hadley?"

Faye stood next to Brad. "She's in a play. She has three performances today."

"Are you going to any?" asked the detective.

"Of course we are. Her final show tonight."

Brad throttled a groan. Without a doubt, they'd see those two at the school auditorium that evening. "If that's all, we'll see you to the door."

They didn't budge. "Does 'Angel Eyes' mean anything to you?"

Brad and Faye exchanged a confused glance.

"Should it?" he asked.

"Just asking." The detective looked at her tablet. "One more thing — what can you tell me about the Valderdorf knife?"

He jolted. It was one of BlueBlade's rarest and most expensive knives, with a distinctive curve to the blade, mostly purchased by collectors. That had to have been the one used to kill Duke. No other reason they'd bring it up. "It's one of my company's knives. Why?"

The two officers exchanged yet another look.

Sergeant Lewis handed him her card. "Call me if you think of anything that might be helpful."

No response before he ushered them outside.

He closed the door and turned to his son.

Zeke's face paled, and he raced up the stairs.

"This just keeps getting better," Brad said.

"I'll talk to him."

"And I'll take care of everything else." He trudged up the stairs, pressure like a gathering storm behind his temples.

Chapter Eight

HADLEY HELD HER BREATH, bracing herself for the final scene.

Every seat was filled, and her entire family was there — even Dad. She'd barely been able to hold herself together through the trio of performances. Her saving grace was being able to throw herself into her character's world. It moved her mind away from everything back home. With her emotions this raw, she was able to give more to her character. Bonus for her performance.

And everyone had taken note. The teacher — and most of the students — had commented on how she'd saved her best for last.

"Hadley!" Ellie tugged on her costume.

She shook her head to clear it. Realized everyone was getting into place. Forced a smile. "Just getting into the right headspace."

Her thoughts struggled for her attention. She needed to focus on the scene — which she knew well enough to do in her sleep — but she couldn't stop thinking about Duke. *Dead.*

The curtains opened, and she forced aside any extraneous thought. In a matter of minutes, she could put this all behind her. Lock herself in her room and blast music. She just needed a good excuse to get out of the celebration afterward. Or maybe she'd have to put on another performance before heading home.

Once the bright lights kicked on, her attention snapped to the play. Waited for the first few lines, belted hers out at just the right moment, and glided across the stage with ease. A few more lines before her solo song.

She'd nailed it all day, and she'd do it again. Two more characters' lines, and then she was up. One more. It was an entire paragraph.

Against her better judgment, she scanned the audience, finding her parents front and center. Zeke was, of course, staring at a wall instead of paying attention. She turned her attention back to the stage when she saw Duke.

Duke.

Excitement flooded her. Until she realized it wasn't him.

It couldn't be, seeing as he was dead.

Tears misted her eyes.

Someone next to her cleared his throat.

Hadley spun around. Smacked into Ellie. Foreheads clunked together.

Some of the cast members gasped, and a few giggled.

Declan twirled her around so gracefully, it might as well have been part of the script, making up a line that was the perfect opening for her song.

She thanked him with her eyes and belted out the first line.

It came out flawlessly. Better than ever before.

Relief flooded her. She focused on the faces of her cast and the props. Stayed in the moment, moving slowly around the stage as she sang her heart out, losing herself until the last line.

Applause erupted. She paused, expecting it to quiet as quickly as it began.

It didn't.

Several of the other cast members patted her on the back. Ellie said something, but the clapping was too loud. Declan gave her a thumbs-up behind his back, invisible to the audience.

The room finally quieted.

Hadley's cheeks warmed as she smiled a thanks before turning to Ellie and delivering the wrong line, forcing her costar to improvise by blending her next two lines to make sense of Hadley's fumble.

She needed to pull herself together. She could make or break this final scene.

This would be what everyone blogged about later.

No pressure.

Declan and Lucy began their song, giving Hadley a moment to collect herself.

The last tune ended, and Hadley jumped in with her line. The final few minutes went off without a single mistake.

The audience gave a standing ovation as the curtain fell. Everything was a blur as the cast hurried to the other side of the stage for their bow. The applause continued so long, they bent over more than a dozen times.

Mrs. Hargrove came out and handed roses to everyone as the clapping continued.

Eventually, everyone finally headed off the stage, trading congratulations on a job well done. They'd practiced for over a month, and all of their efforts had paid off.

Hadley led her classmates out to the hallway, where all the families waited for their stars. Parents of kids who didn't even have lines gushed over them like they'd been the star of the show. It took her a moment to find her parents.

Dad handed her a bouquet of multi-colored roses and smashed her in an embrace. "That was the performance of a lifetime!"

She tried to return the hug, but he was squeezing too tightly. When he let go, she straightened her dress. "But I messed up a couple lines and—"

"And nothing. You were the best one up there."

Luna bounced around, tugging on Hadley. "You're famous!"

Hadley pulled her into her arms. "Maybe someday."

"You are." Luna snuggled against her.

Mom was next, and even Zeke hugged her, both congratulating her on a job well done. They spoke for a few minutes before Ellie and Lucy tugged on Hadley's arms.

"Everyone's leaving for the party. Come on!" She turned to Hadley's parents. "Hi, Mr. and Mrs. Morris."

Mom smiled. "Hello, girls."

"What party?" Dad lifted a brow.

Hadley groaned. "It's not really a party. We're having dinner at McMurphy's Grill. I know I told you."

"Are there going to be boys?"

"*Dad.*" She shoved him and gave Mom a hug. "I'll see you guys in a few hours."

Someone seeming obviously out of place caught her attention behind her parents. The lady officer who had been at their house in the morning.

Hadley stepped toward her friends. "Let's go. Now."

The officer raised her hand and hurried over.

"See you later." Hadley blew kisses at her family and turned around.

"Hadley!" said the cop.

She swore under her breath.

Ellie tilted her head.

"I'll catch up with you," Hadley said.

"What's that about?"

Hadley mouthed *later* before turning around to the officer with a forced smile. "Yes? What are you doing here?" she asked before the woman could respond.

She kept her attention on Hadley. "I'm Detective Carla Stewart, Hadley. My partner and I asked your family some questions earlier, but you weren't there. Do you have a moment?"

Dad stepped between them, his back to Hadley. "Leave her alone. She's on her way to celebrate with her friends for a job well done."

The detective looked around Dad. "It's only a couple of quick questions about your neighbor."

A lump formed in Hadley's throat, blocking any words. Not that she had any.

Dad moved in front of Detective Stewart again. "Now isn't the time."

Hadley pulled herself together. "It's fine, Dad." She maneuvered around him. "I don't know anything. I was performing last night. It's been a busy weekend. Ask anyone here."

"How well did you know Duke Hill?"

She couldn't help a guilty glance at Dad before answering. "No more than any other neighbor."

"Meaning?"

"I'm so busy with school and my other activities, I don't have time to get to know anyone. He seemed like a nice guy. Can I go now?"

She offered her card. "Let me know if you think of anything. You can text that number."

Hadley's pulse quickened.

"Okay. But I don't know anything." She took the card and headed backstage to gather her things.

Behind her, Dad said something about an attorney.

Hadley blinked back tears. She could hold it together just a little longer. Laughing with friends would be the perfect distraction until she could get home.

She found her things and stuck the card in her purse, though it belonged in the trash. Then she looked around before pulling out her cell phone to read over last night's texts from her boyfriend.

Maverick: Miss you. Wish I could be in the audience tonight.

Hadley: Miss you more! You already saw two performances. That's more than anyone else.

Maverick: Still not enough. Break a leg!

Hadley: Thanks. Love you, my Maverick.

Maverick: Love you more, Angel Eyes. Can't wait to see you tonight.

Then Duke had sent a picture of himself making a kissing face.

It simultaneously warmed and shattered her heart.

They hadn't seen each other when she got home from her play. She'd called and texted repeatedly but never got any answer.

Because he had been dead.

And the cops probably knew everything. They had to have his cell phone.

They probably thought she was guilty. That had to be why the detective wanted to talk to her.

She might need that lawyer Dad was talking about.

Chapter Nine

Brad filled a mug with coffee but didn't bother with creamer. It was a black coffee morning. And he was still waiting to hear from his boss. It wasn't unusual for Kurt to be harder to reach on the weekends, but the man was practically avoiding him.

It wasn't Brad's fault that the guy next door had been murdered at almost exactly the same time he'd been taking care of his target. Brad's kill was legit, though. Duke had been annoying and stuck-up as hell, but it wasn't like the guy deserved what happened to him. And, of course, he was offed with a Valderdorf.

The evidence all pointed to him. Apparently, his neighbors all thought that, in Brad's eyes, the stupid fireworks displays were worth killing a man over. No, he went after pedophiles, serial killers, drug dealers, and the like. People who *needed* to be taken down for the sake of a safe society.

Footsteps sounded behind him.

He shoved aside his concerns and offered Faye a smile. "Morning, beautiful."

"Stop." She waved him off and filled her own mug.

"I mean it."

"No, you don't." She sat down and sipped her drink.

"You're as gorgeous as the day I first saw you."

"When I was fourteen, in my cheerleading uniform?"

"You're like a fine wine, improving with time."

She sighed. "Are the investigators still next door?"

"The police tape is still up, but I didn't see any vehicles outside."

"I can't believe he's dead."

"It's shocking, to say the least."

Faye rubbed her eyes. "Do you think we need to worry about our safety? Was the murderer after him specifically, or could he hit us next?"

"There has never been any serious crime in the neighborhood. I'm sure it isn't anything to worry about. What we do need to be concerned about is the cops' interest in our family."

"What if they find out he was here?" she asked, setting her mug down.

"I don't see how. Not after we removed the footage from the cloud. They can't prove anything."

"What if someone else's camera caught it?"

"I did some reading last night, and most of these don't store the images for long before they're replaced with new footage."

"But it seems like someone could've gotten something. Can't they save it?"

"Sure. *If* they captured anything." He rested his hand on hers. "I looked around yesterday, and given the way the homes are spaced, I really don't think any of the doorbell cams are pointed anywhere near our front yard."

"What if someone has other cameras? Like the Johnstons. That woman is paranoid about everything."

"Let's not worry about it. We have enough to think about as it is."

Brad pulled out his phone and checked the news. Duke's murder was all anyone locally was talking about — that was no surprise — but there weren't many details. Nothing about the knife or anyone the police were questioning.

So far, so good. He just needed to talk with his boss, who had promised to help, but so far had done nothing.

He should've heard something by now.

Brad rose. "I'm going to call Kurt again."

Faye shifted in her seat. "I need to ask you something. It'll be quick."

Her tone made his stomach knot. "What did I do now?"

"Nothing." She patted his chair.

"What is it, then?" He sat.

"It has nothing to do with the police or our kids."

"Okay. And for the record, I don't like those two groups in the same sentence."

She halfway smiled. "I think we should host the neighborhood Super Bowl party."

He blinked a few times. "Come again?"

"The party."

"Tonight? Here?"

Faye nodded. "I'll recruit the kids to help clean. It'll be fine."

Images of nosy neighbors rummaging through their things flashed through his mind. People who wanted to prove him guilty of killing Duke. Given the way some of them had eyed him outside, and at the play yesterday, they would probably be thrilled to capitalize on the situation.

"Brad?"

He snapped his attention back to her. "No."

"No?"

"There's no way we're hosting the party. It's asking for trouble."

She twisted hair around her finger. "Or it would show the neighbors how hospitable we are."

"Meaning?"

"Everyone has been looking forward to Duke's party."

"Not me."

"Of course not." Faye drew in a deep breath. "But it would be an act of goodwill to host the party. Give the neighborhood a place where everyone can come together and mourn."

He shook his head.

"It would help put us in a good light. You have to admit we could use a little of that. A lot, actually."

More images raced through his mind. This time, of people breaking into his office and finding everything he had at the house for his job — not only the knives but the tools of his profession. "I get where you're coming from, but it really isn't a good idea."

"Why don't you want people in our house?"

Anger churned in his gut. "We have parties."

"You mean the summertime barbecues?"

"Right. It's perfect. Those keep people outside."

Her brows drew together. "Why don't you want people in here? Not for a simple party and not for me to have my dream of an in-home salon?"

"Not that again."

"Why don't you want people in here? It's not like we have anything to hide!"

Brad gritted his teeth. He hated keeping the truth from her at all, and he would never lie about anything outside of his job, but he had to keep his cover.

No exceptions.

"What aren't you telling me?" She pressed her palms on the table.

He closed his eyes a moment before meeting her gaze. "You know me. I value privacy. And having everyone over tonight will only invite people to snoop."

"And what exactly would they find? We aren't guilty, Brad. And they all think you hated him. What better way to show them how wrong they are?"

"Because I don't want our entire neighborhood traipsing through our house!"

"They wouldn't be. Everyone would be in the living room watching the game."

"Everyone?" he countered.

She took several small breaths. "I'm sure a bunch of the wives will be in the dining room, enjoying the snacks. And we could set up games for the kids in the front sitting room. It'll be fine."

"You can guarantee nobody will go upstairs?"

Her mouth curved down. "No, I can't *guarantee* it. But it isn't like we have anything to hide."

If only. "We have plenty to steal."

"Now you're worried that we're surrounded by a pack of thieves?"

"That's what we're opening ourselves up to if we invite a bunch of strangers. Some of whom apparently see us as capable of murder."

"You," she mumbled.

"I'm done discussing this. No parties." Brad hurried out of the room.

He marched up the stairs and stopped at his office. Typed the code into the lockbox he'd installed long ago and collapsed onto his leather chair, his heart racing.

How could Faye think hosting a party would be a good idea? That would be crazy, even without knowing his secrets. Nearly every finger was pointed at him, and she was crazy to think *that no one* would snoop.

An outside noise nabbed his attention. Probably someone dragging garbage to the curb. Despite the HOA rules, there was always one wise guy who put them out way too early.

But the sounds continued for several minutes, so he pulled himself from the chair and glanced out the blinds.

About half a dozen people gathered in front of Duke's house. Not nearly the crowd from yesterday, but enough to spark his curiosity.

One lady — Brad couldn't remember her name, but she was always spouting off her opinions at the meetings — turned and pointed to his house. Almost at his window.

Brad lowered the blind slightly, but kept watching. The group seemed deep in conversation, shifting their attention back and forth between his house and Duke's.

Each time they turned his way, literally pointing fingers, they looked annoyed.

No, not annoyed. *Suspicious.*

They had to be cooking up theories, figuring out how he would have offed their neighbor.

He needed to know what they were saying. But there was no way to hear from inside the house, and he sure wasn't going out there to talk with them.

Not only that, but if he didn't hear back from Kurt soon, he might have to launch his own investigation to find out who really killed Duke.

He pulled out his phone, used voice command to make the call, and got his boss' voicemail. So he called again. But still no answer.

There was only one thing to do. He would have to tell Faye that he would go along with the party, but only on the condition that they lock up their valuables. And while his family was busy doing that, he would make sure his office lock's code was updated.

Brad went out into the hall and tried to change the code. It had been too long, and he couldn't remember the procedure, so he needed to find the paperwork. After nearly twenty wasted minutes, he finally had a new code.

He passed Hadley on his way to Faye. "Mom wants to have the Super Bowl party here. We need to start picking up."

Her mouth gaped. "We're hosting? Tonight?"

"I suggest locking up your valuables. I don't trust any of these people." Brad checked his phone as he darted down the stairs.

But still nothing from Kurt.

He would have to go to work and deal with Kurt face to face.

Then he'd worry about his nosy neighbors going through his house, looking for evidence to prove that he was a murderer.

Chapter Ten

BRAD GLANCED around the sparse parking lot. Kurt's car wasn't there, but he fretted every scratch when driving his convertible and might have parked around back.

He set the alarm and hurried into the knife shop. A new kid stood behind the counter. Brad couldn't remember his name. But he looked too jumpy to be anywhere near weapons.

Not his call or his concern. Finding his boss was a singular mission.

"Hey." The kid gave a half-hearted wave and an even less enthusiastic smile.

Brad nodded as he made his way to the back room.

Ghost town.

"Where is everyone?" He kicked a candy wrapper out of the way.

"It's the day of the big game," came a feminine voice from behind.

Rose. Though she'd been with the company for several years now, she still acted like she had too much to prove. She'd be a loose cannon until she got that under control.

He'd tried when training her, but she had some deeper issues that went beyond the scope of his job or interest — always going against what he said or trying to show him up. Once trained, she'd grown even worse.

"Right." Brad looked behind her. "Kurt in?"

"Nope. I think he's hosting a party tonight for his hoity-toity friends." She licked chocolate off her finger, then tucked some of her long, dark hair behind her ear. "What brings you in?"

None of your business.

"What about Ralf?" he asked.

Ralf Bergmann was Kurt's father and still the head of the company in his mid-seventies.

Rose snorted. "Right. He comes in, what, once a quarter now?"

Brad passed her and knocked on Bergmann's door. Turned the locked knob. Muttered under his breath.

"Anything I can help you with?" Rose gave him a sultry smile.

"No."

"I'm resourceful, you know."

"You can't help with this." He called Kurt again. No surprise, his call went to voicemail.

Rose pulled out a chair. "Have a seat. Unburden yourself."

He didn't budge. Needed to figure something out. Couldn't wait until the next day.

"I heard you ran into trouble on your last job."

Brad glared at her. "Some guys jumped me, and my target nearly got away. You could call that trouble."

"But you *did* get him." She sat next to the empty chair, slowly crossing one long leg over the other.

"Of course! That's what I do."

"Then why so upset?"

Pressure built behind his temples as he sat in the stiff plastic chair. "My neighbor was murdered."

Her lips parted, and she rested her hand on his. "Were you close?"

Brad pulled his hand away. "No. That's the problem. Some of my neighbors seem to think I did it. Those neighbors not only told the cops, they're discussing theories."

"If you didn't do it, that should be easy enough to prove."

"Right, I'll just tell them I was killing someone else at the time."

"Oh, my." Rose covered her mouth.

"Yeah. Not exactly the alibi of the century."

"What did you say?" She leaned forward, exposing her cleavage.

He looked up at a rare knife hanging on the wall — even rarer than the one used to kill Duke. "My *wife* said we were together. Dinner and a movie alone. Nobody to vouch for us."

"I can."

"What?" He turned back to her.

She nodded quickly. "I was on a job, too. Send them to me. I can say we ran into each other getting food. It's perfect. You'll be off the hook."

"I'll think about it. Don't say anything until I can figure out how that can work into our story, which probably involves a cabin in the woods."

"Probably?"

"The details aren't hashed out yet." He cringed, feeling like an idiot. If Faye hadn't blurted her story, he could've come up with something legit. That's one of the things he was best at.

"Let me know if I can help."

"Kurt said he was working on something, but he hasn't gotten back to me."

"That's not like him. But it *is* Super Bowl Sunday."

"I could be charged with murder, but all anyone wants to talk about is the game."

She cocked a brow. "Are you going to a party tonight?"

"My wife wants to *host* a party. She thinks it'll put us in a good light for the neighbors since the dead guy was originally going to have it at his place. Obviously, that's off."

They shared a chuckle, and Brad finally began to relax. It was nice to be around someone who understood his comfort with death.

Rose glanced to the side before meeting his gaze. "I have an idea."

"To help with my situation?"

"Exactly. I'll come to your party — maybe bring a few guys from work."

He stifled a groan. "How's that supposed to help?"

"Don't you get it?" She batted her eyes. "I can put in a good word for you — talk loudly about how great it was running into you two Friday night. And even better, I can grill your neighbors for deets. Since I don't know any of them, it would make perfect sense for me to ask questions. I wouldn't be nosy, I'd be friendly, curious."

Instinctively, he wanted to object, but the idea had merit. "It could work."

She gave him a playful shove. "Stop. You know it's genius. What do you want me to bring?"

"Huh?"

"Appetizers. Everyone brings food to these things. It'd raise eyebrows if I showed up empty-handed."

"Oh, right. I have no idea. Faye is planning the party."

"I'll figure something out." She rested her hand on his arm. "Go home and get ready for the party. I'll take care of your alibi and questioning the neighbors. All you have to do is show everyone what a friendly guy you are."

"That still doesn't fix my problem of not being able to reach Kurt."

"I wouldn't worry about that. He'll be back in the morning — unless he has a hangover." She snickered. "But by the time I've spoken with your neighbors, you won't need Kurt."

That was doubtful, but he nodded. At this point, he needed all the help he could get. And his neighbors would be more willing to talk to Rose than to him. If he started questioning people, they would get defensive and close right up.

"What do you say?"

"Okay. I appreciate the help."

"My pleasure." She leaped from the chair and nudged him. "Besides, I was looking for a party."

He forced a smile. "Great."

"Go on. I'll see you tonight."

He hurried to his car. Maybe with Rose's help, they could find the real killer.

If that person had the nerve to make an appearance at the party.

Chapter Eleven

FAYE STUCK another batch of cookies into the oven and wiped her forehead. Outside, she could see part of Duke's backyard. The edge of a porch swing and part of his apple tree. He used to bring over bags of apples for her to make pies.

She felt a sting of guilt for hosting the party. Maybe it was a bad idea so close to his death. Would the neighbors think it was in poor taste?

Everyone had been friendly enough when she'd invited them, but what if they really saw her as heartless? Maybe she should've listened to Brad when he first said no.

Too late now.

Ding-dong!

She glanced at the time. The party wasn't due to start for more than a couple of hours. She set the timer and hurried to the front door, brushing her face in case there were flour smears.

Outside the window, Allison Campbell balanced a container of food in one hand while she adjusted some Panther streamers hanging from the porch.

Faye opened the door. "Allison, what a surprise. I wasn't expecting anyone yet."

Allison turned and smiled widely, brushing some wavy blonde hair behind her shoulder. "I thought you could use some help. You know, since this party was sprung on you last minute and all. And I brought my famous bean dip. Hope you have chips."

Faye was glad for the help. With Brad at work, everything was on her. "I'm sure someone will bring some. Come on in."

Allison sniffed dramatically in the entry. "Mmm. Smells delicious. Snickerdoodles?"

"Yes. How'd you know?"

She tapped her nose. "I'm a baking expert."

"Fantastic." Faye took the food and led her to the kitchen.

"I didn't realize you have the same layout as us. Does the main bathroom upstairs bother you? Wes never stops complaining about it being too far from the bedrooms."

"Nope. No problems." Faye set the dip down. Hopefully, Allison wouldn't mention anything more about never having been in the house.

"What do you need help with? I'll do anything — decorations or clean up."

Did the house need cleaning? She usually kept it up and thought it looked fine, but now she was inspecting the room for any missed dust. "I was just going to blow up some balloons. Do you think that's enough decoration?"

"That's it? Given how elaborate everything is outside, I think the neighborhood is probably expecting something phenomenal in here. Duke went all out."

"Like you said, we weren't planning on hosting this. I only thought of it this morning."

"Too bad we can't get inside Duke's."

Faye gasped.

"Too soon? Sorry." Allison sat at the island and tapped her perfectly manicured nails. "Maybe Brittany has something? It would all be Seahawks, though."

"I think people will understand if we don't have—"

"This has to be special. We're here to lift morale. Everyone is so glum about the murder."

"A party isn't going to change that." Faye turned off the timer a second ahead of its ringing and took out the cookies. "I can check the garage. Brad might have some stuff he didn't put out this year."

"Wait! I have the perfect idea. Joey had a football-themed birthday party a year or two ago. I hung onto everything — just in case." Allison rubbed her loose-fitting shirt.

"You're expecting?"

"Six months. Another boy." She beamed, then the smile quickly faded. "But I'm huge this time."

Faye choked on air. "I couldn't even tell."

"You're too sweet, but I'm big as a whale. Anyway, I'll be back in a few minutes with those decorations."

"You really don't have to. Please, don't go out of your way."

"Nonsense, I'll be right back," Allison said. "If you're done with the oven, you'll want to put the dip in there to keep warm."

She left the room with an elegant grace.

Faye stared after her for a moment. How could she be six months along? When Faye had been that far, she was waddling and swollen everywhere — not to mention her beach ball-sized belly.

She turned back to the counter, counted the cookies, decided they had enough, then put the bean dip in the oven.

The front door opened and closed.

"Faye?" Brad called.

"In here!" She pulled out her favorite recipe book and flipped through the pages, looking for anything potentially delicious that she already had the ingredients to make.

He paused in the doorway, his hair slightly disheveled. "Why was Allison here?"

They must've run into each other out front.

"She's helping," Faye replied without looking up.

"With what?"

"The party." She stopped at a page for cheese and bacon tater tot skewers. That seemed easy enough to whip up.

"Why her?"

"She showed up." Faye dug around the pantry for skewers and seasoning.

Brad groaned. "At least she left."

"Not for long. She's coming back with decorations for inside the house."

"I could've picked something up on my way."

Faye glanced back. "It was her idea."

"Of course it was."

"What's that supposed to mean?"

He threw her an exasperated look. "Are you kidding? The woman is just trying to make me look incompetent."

"That isn't true, Brad. She only wants to help."

"She always comes over to put the decorations outside."

"Allison's a little pushy, I'll admit, but she just likes giving people ideas to make whatever they're doing better."

"I don't like her being here."

Faye crossed her arms, defensiveness blooming in her chest. "I wasn't about to turn her away. It wasn't like I was getting help from anyone else."

"You could've asked the kids. And now I'm here. What do you need me to do?"

"Help Allison hang the decorations?"

"That isn't happening." Brad threw his arms in the air. "I'm going to send the kids down here. *They* can help her while I check the garage for anything I have that'll work. If she makes one remark about me wanting Duke dead, I'm kicking her out of our house."

"She won't."

"I'll believe it when I see it."

"Remember, we're hosting this party to show everyone how hospitable we can be. That means putting our best foot forward. Kicking Allison Campbell out is the opposite of that."

He scowled. "She has it coming."

"Why do you think she's so bad? She suggested we use Duke's decorations."

"She did? That sounds like something I'd say."

"Exactly. Give her a chance. She really isn't as bad as you think."

"I'm not holding my breath, but I can promise to try."

"Thank you."

"I'm more interested in finding out who the real killer is anyway." He went upstairs, calling for the kids to help their mother.

Faye turned to the fridge and gathered the rest of her ingredients.

It was going to be one long night.

Chapter Twelve

CRASH!

Brad whipped around, his skin hot with irritation.

Mitch, from down the street, picked up a lamp next to the couch. "Ha-ha. Trevor is so rambunctious. No harm, no foul."

"Right." Brad forced a smile while shoving his fists into his pockets.

Pretending to be nice to several dozen people who thought he was a murderer for an entire evening might just kill him.

But if he could nail down some actual suspects, everything would be worth it. So far, Brad had nothing.

The night was still young, with the pre-game show winding down. It seemed like half the neighborhood was in his house, and more were still coming. He'd been eyeing the stairs since Allison arrived with her armload of streamers and decorative paper footballs. So far, everyone was being good and staying where they belonged.

He almost wished someone would try and sneak up. It would be the perfect opportunity to confront somebody.

Two little boys ran in his direction, screaming at the top of their lungs. The smaller one smashed into Brad's legs, backed up, and chased after the other one with a screech high-pitched enough to crack glass.

Brad drew in a deep breath and walked around, nodding and smiling at neighbors. Giving the good impression Faye wanted and listening to conversations just as he had planned to.

Duke was the subject of some discussion, but so far, nobody had been dumb enough to mention Brad, at least not within earshot.

Could that mean nobody actually believed him capable of killing his innocent neighbor? It would be so much easier to find the real criminal without all those fingers pointing at him.

Faye waved him into the kitchen and placed a platter of football-shaped sandwiches in his arms. "Offer these to the guests. Don't forget to smile."

"I *am* smiling. Even when Mitch's kid knocked over your grandma's lamp."

Faye's eyes widened.

"It's fine. No harm, no foul." Brad impressed himself with an imitation of their neighbor.

"Pass those out. And compliment people."

"Now you want me to give fake flattery?"

"They'll see right through it if you're phony. Find something you genuinely like. A haircut, nice shirt, *something*."

He cringed at the thought. "Fine."

"Or at least ask questions about their lives. People like those who seem interested in them. It's a law of nature."

"If it'll help stop the accusations, I'm all in." He shuddered.

"They'll genuinely like you if you give them an opportunity."

Brad headed back to the living room, offering the platter to everyone he passed. There were at least twice as many guests as there had been a few minutes before. He tried to find something nice to say about the first few people who took the mini sandwiches but found nothing. Donna Brown, from one street over, had a ridiculous haircut that looked like her toddler had done it blindfolded. Larry Davis was decked out in Seahawk gear, despite the local team not even making the first round of the playoffs.

How was he supposed to suck up to these people? It was like they were trying to be off-putting.

Brad placed the platter on the coffee table between other snacks and checked the TV. The announcers were discussing their views on how the game would play out.

Good. That meant the game would start soon.

He was already itching to get everyone out of his house. But on the bright side, he had at least four hours to question people. Maybe by the end of the night, he'd have at least one good suspect.

Out of habit, he kept glancing over every time the door opened. He didn't know what made his skin crawl more — the adults and their suspicious eyes or the kids running around, crashing into things.

He wandered around, making small talk and offering compliments like Faye suggested. It did seem to put some of their guests at ease, but others held their accusatory stares.

It was those he needed to focus on. If saying nice things didn't work, he'd have to find some other way to loosen them up. Or straight-up ask where they were at the time of the murder. That would also work.

Shortly after kickoff, familiar voices sounded at the entry. Rose, who had brought several guys from the shop with her. Justin, Roger, Dillon, and that kid from earlier were all making their way to the living room.

He hurried over and welcomed them, offering a tray of cheese and crackers he'd grabbed from the coffee table.

"Where can I put this?" Rose asked, raising her bowl.

Faye appeared beside him. "Snack or main dish?"

"Salad."

"I'll take it to the kitchen for now. I'm Faye."

"Rose Flores. It's so nice to finally meet you." She handed the bowl over. "Brad has told us all so much about you."

"Oh, you're from BlueBlade?"

"Yes." Rose flashed her brightest smile. "We all look up to Brad. Hard not to when he's so high up in the company."

Faye gave him an approving look. "That's great to hear. Make yourself at home."

"Has the game already started?" Dillon hurried to the living room, and the other guys followed.

Rose pulled Brad to the side. "Anyone you want me to talk to first?"

"You could start with the people glaring at me. I can't get a word from any of them."

She straightened her back, sticking out her chest. "I'm on it. And don't worry, we'll find the real killer whether they're here or not. All of these people are neighbors?"

"Unfortunately."

"Great. This'll be fun. Just relax and enjoy your party." She put her hand on his arm, near his chest. "If I find something useful, you could put in a good word with Kurt for me."

"Sure, no problem."

"Great. I like making people sweat." She winked and sauntered toward the living room.

He turned to see Faye watching.

She cleared her throat. "She seems nice."

"Rose wants to help. That's why she's here."

"Help with what?"

Brad stepped closer. "Finding the murderer. Nobody will talk to me."

"Why did you ask for her help?" Faye shifted, adjusting her shirt and glancing toward the main part of the party.

"I didn't. She volunteered."

"Really? How'd she know about Duke?"

"I ran into her at the office earlier. Couldn't find Kurt."

"So you told her that the police suspect you?"

"Yes. I was frustrated, and she could tell. Look, we're wasting time here. It's going to be much harder after this. We have to take advantage of everyone being in one place."

She frowned. "Okay. Let me know if you learn anything."

He kissed her on the cheek. "Will do. And don't worry about Rose. She's harmless."

"If you say so. As long as this isn't a repeat of Jessica Witten."

Brad drew in a measured breath, carefully considering his words. "I can't believe you're bringing that up. And like I said, Rose only wants to help. I think she's just excited to be at a party."

"Somehow, I find it hard to believe that she'd have trouble landing an invite."

"Kurt isn't doing anything for me right now. At least she wants to help. She's great at her job."

"Selling knives?"

"Yes. It takes more skill than you'd think."

"I hope you're right." Faye's mouth formed a straight line before she spun around and marched into the kitchen.

Irritation ran through him, but he pushed it aside. He would have to deal with Faye later.

Rose had a group of husbands gathered around her in the living room, all of them laughing at something she said.

Was that her way of trying to pull a confession? It looked more like she was ready to pass out shots.

At least if Faye looked in, that sight would put her mind at ease. Then they wouldn't need to discuss either Rose or Jessica.

How could she bring that up again after so long?

Chapter Thirteen

BRAD GRABBED a beer from a cooler and took a quick swig. Just enough to ease his frayed nerves. He needed to be clear-headed to question those who would talk to him.

Fallon, one of several millennials who occupied the only rental house in the subdivision, grabbed a beer too. "Cool party."

"Too bad about Duke."

"Yeah. I wonder what he did to piss someone off bad enough to kill him."

Brad took a sip. "No idea. Did you know him well?"

"Nope. Dude never talked about anything other than trying to get me into his pyramid business."

"Exactly." Brad gave him an easy smile. "Wasn't he about your age?"

Fallon shrugged. "Maybe. He acted like an old married guy — no offense."

"None taken."

"He wasn't one of us, is all I'm saying. You won't see us decorating for the holidays."

"It isn't for everyone." Brad finished his drink. He was

69

slightly more relaxed but could really use another. He just wasn't willing to risk falling off his game.

"So, what made you want to have the party here? I mean, aside from the fact that Duke obviously can't."

"Why not? Our house already looks the part."

"I guess." Fallon poked one of Allison's decorations. "But I mean, with everyone wondering if you did it."

"What kind of lunatic would kill a man over decorations?"

"Got me."

Cassidy, one of Fallon's roommates, came over. "Whatcha talking about?"

"Whether or not he killed Duke over the decorations."

"Oh my gosh. You can't say that to his face!" Her cheeks reddened as she turned to Brad. "It's just gossip. Nobody believes it. Fallon can be an idiot."

"Shut up."

"I can handle a little gossip," Brad said. "What do you think?"

"Me?" Cassidy's hands went to her neck. "I don't... I mean ... You seem like a nice guy. Your kids never get into trouble."

Brad leaned against the wall. "You think it's a possibility?"

"No. That's insane."

Fallon grabbed another beer. "Where *were* you that night?"

Cassidy glowered at him.

"Me?" Brad pointed at his chest. "I was on a date with my lovely wife."

"Who says lovely wife? Sounds like a cover to me."

Brad's heart gathered speed. He wasn't about to let this punk get the best of him. "Mature adults talk like that. Something you clearly don't understand."

"I'm so sorry," Cassidy mouthed before turning to Fallon. "Come on. Let's ease up. You already had those wine coolers at home."

Brad smirked.

Fallon flipped him off.

"What was I saying about maturity?"

Lane, another of their roommates, came over. "What's up?"

Fallon set his drink down. "We were just trying to figure out where Brad was the night Duke died."

"Interesting. Where?"

"He says on a date with his lovely wife." Fallon's tone dripped with sarcasm.

"So sweet." Lane smiled.

"Can you prove anything?" Fallon demanded.

"What do I need to prove to you?" Brad stared him down. "The police know all the details, and yet here I am. No cuffs. What about you?"

"What about me?"

"Where were *you* the night Duke died?"

"At a frat party. It was tight. Lots of people to vouch for me. Who can do the same for you?"

Brad resisted the urge to grab another drink. No way would he let this guy get to him. Wasn't going to happen. "Slow down on the drinks. There are kids running around."

"Sorry about him." Cassidy put her hands on Fallon's shoulders. "If he doesn't calm down, I'll see him home."

"It'd beat being here." Fallon stomped off.

"Enjoy the appetizers," Brad said through gritted teeth before walking away.

"You okay?" Lucas had snuck up on him from behind.

"No dog?" Brad asked, looking for the chihuahua.

"Mitzy's at home sleeping. Being around this much noise really sets off her anxiety."

"Of course." Brad looked around for someone suspicious to question. Lucas was annoying but hardly the murderous type.

Rose was laughing with a different group of guys. Maybe she was on to something, getting people to loosen up like that. He'd accomplished nothing with that fool a moment ago.

"What was Fallon mouthing off about now?" Lucas asked.

Brad turned back to him. "What? Oh, he seems to think I'm guilty of murder."

"I wouldn't put it past *him*." Lucas leaned closer. "You didn't hear this from me, but he and Duke have never gotten along. Like, ever."

"Really?"

"Duke brought over a fruit basket and wine when those kids rented the Clairborne house. Fallon nearly punched him. I thought it was going to get ugly, but Duke walked away while Fallon shouted obscenities. It was awful — I had to cover Mitzy's ears."

"Did you tell the police about that?"

Lucas nodded slowly, glancing over at their temperamental neighbor. "They know."

"And yet he's still walking free?"

"Solid alibi. Not that drunk college kids are trustworthy, but he claims to be in a bunch of selfies and videos. All posted to social media, apparently."

"It pays to be a narcissist."

"And he doesn't have the brainpower to pull off a hit. Oh, look. Tristan's here. I'm so glad he got off work." Lucas bounced toward the door, turning back toward Brad to say, "Talk to you later!"

Brad made a mental note to check into Fallon's alibi. It was likely to hold up, given the cops already knew, but a closer look wouldn't hurt, especially if it could get him off the hook.

"Everything okay?" Allison gave him a bright smile.

Bile rose in his mouth. "Great. Having fun?"

"The *best* time."

"If you get tired, don't feel bad about leaving early. We'll return your decorations."

"I'm great." She stepped closer. "I couldn't help over-hearing your discussion with Fallon."

"He's drunk on wine coolers."

"Were you really on a date with Faye the other night?"

"Yes. Why do you ask?"

Allison picked a piece of fuzz from her Steelers jersey. "I was busy running errands all evening, and I swear Faye's car was—"

"We took mine."

"Did you?"

"It's roomier."

She tilted her head. "Why do you have the nicer car?"

"Excuse me?"

"Usually, husbands let their wives drive the better car. Not you."

"What are you trying to say?"

"Do I need to spell it out?"

"No. And not that I owe you an explanation, Faye's car *is* the more expensive one. It has more safety features than mine."

"Thinking of the kids, I'm sure. Did you pick it out for her? Or did she get a say?"

Brad marched away, counting silently to twenty. That woman needed to mind her own business. She'd hardly said two words to either of them in months, and now suddenly she was Faye's guardian angel?

She was only trying to get under his skin. And same as with Fallon, he wasn't going to let her.

Donna stepped in front of him, running a hand through her uneven hairstyle. "Great party."

"Glad you approve."

Her expression stiffened. "I heard you say that you drove your car the night of the murder?"

"Yes. Exciting, isn't it?"

"It's interesting because I would swear I saw your car behind the knife shop."

Brad narrowed his eyes. "You were back there?"

"Was it your car? Or one that looks exactly like it?"

"What were you doing behind the store?"

"Pardon me?" Donna asked with puppy eyes.

"The back lot can't be seen from the road or the main parking area. You have to drive all the way around the building and weave through a maze of dumpsters and a narrow alley."

"What's your point?"

"I want to know why you were back there. If you *were* there, it wasn't by accident."

She raised her voice. "Why are you getting so defensive, Brad?"

Several people turned their way.

"Defensive? I'm asking a legitimate question. You're the one refusing to answer."

"Did you take your wife on a date to your work?"

A few others glanced their way.

He clenched his jaw, counted to ten. "That's insane."

"If Faye's car was here all night and yours was at your work, where did you take your lovely wife on a date at the same time Duke was murdered?"

A pair of neighbors inched closer.

"We took a company car."

"Now we're getting somewhere."

"Because I took one of BlueBlade's vehicles?"

Donna smirked. "Why take a nondescript sedan when you could've painted the town red in that beautiful car you love to show off?"

"I don't love — why do you know so much about my boss's cars?"

Lisa and Sue joined them, both watching Brad.

He kept his focus on Donna. "If you must know, Faye and I went to her parents' cabin. I didn't want to scratch my car."

"You wanted to ruin your boss's?"

"It's already beat up. Who cares?"

Lisa took another step closer. "How far away is the cabin?"

"A half hour? Want me to check my mileage?"

"What time did you go?" Lisa stared him down. "I saw your wife through a window in the front room around seven."

"Impossible."

"Is it?"

"Yes!" Brad exclaimed. "She was with me."

Donna rubbed her chin. "Can you prove it?"

"Of course." He waved toward Rose. "We saw my coworker. She'll tell you all about it. But you'd know that if you were there, wouldn't you?"

"Interesting choice of alibi."

"Choice?"

"If Lisa's right, Faye was here, and you were at work — with that sexy young thing."

"Let's go talk to her." Donna grabbed Lisa and Sue by their arms. "I'm sure her story matches exactly. I just wonder what Faye thinks of it."

"She doesn't care because we were at the cabin!"

All three ladies shot him knowing looks.

"Ask Faye," he said, throttling his urge to plunge a fist into the wall. "She'll tell you."

Brad swallowed hard.

This was getting seriously out of control.

Chapter Fourteen

FAYE'S STOMACH tightened as she watched Brad and Rose whispering across the room. If they stood any closer, their lips might start touching.

"He works with her all day?" Allison rested a hand on her arm.

She pulled her attention from her husband and Rose. "It's a full shop. Mostly guys."

"But still, they're together all day, every day?"

"It isn't like that. And Brad isn't one to flirt."

"Could've fooled me." Allison nibbled a bacon-covered pepper.

"They aren't flirting."

"Maybe not, but they're close. Just look at them."

"No more than any other coworker." That was a stretch, but she wasn't about to admit that to Allison.

"I don't see him standing that close to any of the guys who came with her."

"He also isn't talking to any of them right now. And besides, I trust Brad."

Allison frowned. "I trusted my first husband, too."

Faye gave her a double-take. "You have a first husband?"

"Yeah, and Wes isn't him. Jeff was one of those guys who made all the girls feel like the most special person in the room. I told myself he was just charismatic — someone who could hold a conversation with a doorknob. But then I came home early one day." A dramatic sigh. "The rest is history. Wes and I are happy. That's all that matters."

Acid churned in her gut.

Allison smiled brightly. "But if you've been together a long time and trust him, I'm sure it's fine."

"Since I was fourteen and he was sixteen."

Her mouth fell open. "That long?"

"We've been through everything together. Getting through his dad's murder made us really close. We've stayed tight ever since."

"You obviously know him better than I do. He's never gone out on you before, right?"

"Exactly." Jessica Witten's face sprang to Faye's mind. She hadn't thought about her in more than a decade, and now, twice in one night.

"Perfect. Then Rose is just smitten. He's probably oblivious. You know how guys are."

Faye forced a laugh.

Allison said, "I'm going to check on the pizza. The timer's about to go off. Mingle. It's your party, and you've been in the kitchen the whole time."

"Good idea."

She hated the idea. Taking care of the food kept her away from nosy questions. Every time she spoke about the night of the murder, she was forced into yet another lie. She never should've said she was on a date with Brad. Anyone who knew them would rightly raise eyebrows.

It would've been better if she'd just admitted to having

cut Duke's hair right before his death. It would've been easy enough to prove her innocence, seeing as she had nothing to do with his death.

Would it be better or worse to come clean now?

Worse. Definitely worse. She'd heard Brad telling numerous people about their date. And he'd told her she needed to say they took his car to BlueBlade, where they'd then taken one of the older company cars.

Everything was spiraling.

Allison caught her attention and waved her toward the living room.

Faye joined the guests but then bolted upstairs before speaking to anyone.

Brad met her gaze. No surprise, since he was eyeing the stairs like a hawk, sure someone would go up to rifle through their things or even steal something.

Music sounded down the hall.

She followed it to Hadley's room. Her stomach dropped. She better not have a boy in there; she knew the rules.

Faye turned the knob.

Locked.

She pounded on the door. "Hadley Marie! Open the door!"

Shuffling sounded on the other side before the door flung open. "Mom! Stop."

Faye pushed past her. "Where is he?"

"Who?"

"Whatever boy you have hidden in here?"

"I'm alone!"

She opened the closet and moved her daughter's clothes around. "That's exactly what you'd say if you had a boy in here."

"I *don't*."

Faye looked under the bed. "What are you doing up here?"

"Homework." She pointed to open textbooks on the bed.

"Why?"

"Because I have school tomorrow." Her eyes were red.

"Are you okay?"

"Yeah."

"Come down to the party."

Hadley shook her head. "I have to get this report done."

"The entire neighborhood is here. I think it'd help if you at least make an appearance."

"Help?"

"So many people think Dad could've done it."

Hadley's face paled. "You mean … Duke?"

Faye nodded. "And it doesn't help that the police have questioned us more than anyone else."

"He wouldn't…" She chewed on a nail.

"We know that, but they don't. Just come down and say hi to a few people. There's a lot of food. I'm sure all this studying is building up an appetite."

"Give me a minute to put on some makeup and do something with my hair. Maybe change my clothes."

Faye embraced her. "You look beautiful as you are, but I understand if you want to. Don't feel like you have to stay all night, but please, have some snacks and give your dad a hug. I'm sure he could use it."

"Okay."

"Thanks, honey. It really will help and do you some good."

"I guess."

Faye returned to the party. Only then did it strike her as odd that Hadley looked like she'd been crying. This whole investigation was really throwing her off. She returned to her daughter's room, but the door was already closed, and the music blaring even louder than before.

They'd have a talk after the party. Or maybe Faye would pull her aside downstairs. But at least she'd agreed to join everyone. Maybe that would pull her out of this funk.

Faye went straight to the kitchen and checked the oven, unable to remember if she'd even put anything in it. There was a pizza, and it looked ready, so she took it out and set it on the stove to cool.

"You got it," Allison said, hurrying into the kitchen. "Thanks. Where'd you disappear to?"

"Begging my daughter to come downstairs for a few minutes."

"Luna's running around with — oh, you mean Hadley. Teenagers. It's one drama after another, am I right?"

Faye leaned against the island, sipping from a wine glass. "Yep. Though we've been lucky with Zeke. He's such a good kid. He just plays too many video games."

"He's only fourteen?"

"Right."

Allison smirked. "Plenty of time for his attitude to take over."

"Great."

She gave Faye a friendly shove. "Don't worry about it. They always come around later. You're close to your parents now, right?"

Faye hesitated. She avoided them at all costs, but she also parented the opposite of them, so hopefully, her kids wouldn't run for the hills after graduation.

"No?" Allison poured both of them some sparkling apple cider. "I certainly did. It only took a few weeks at college to make me realize how much I needed my parents."

"I couldn't get enough of the freedom, personally."

"Everyone is different, I suppose."

"Cheers to that." Faye raised her glass.

Allison chuckled. "Cheers."

Applause erupted in the living room, followed by a string of complaints.

Faye set her glass down. "I'm going to see who just scored."

"Pretty sure it was the Panthers."

"How can you tell?"

"Wes was one of the people booing. Lifelong Steelers fan. He only pretends to like the Seahawks during the regular season."

"Gotcha. I'm going to check on Hadley. She should be down by now."

"Go easy on her. It's rougher being a teen than when we were kids." Allison looked lost in thought, her eyes sad.

Faye didn't want to hear whatever story she was obviously supposed to ask about, so she headed into the living room.

Everyone was laughing about a commercial with a talking dog holding a beer.

No Hadley in sight. Maybe she was still getting ready. That girl could spend twenty minutes on her eyes alone.

Faye made her way to the entry, which had turned into a kids' playroom for the evening. Luna had brought down some of her toys, and they were all playing happily. Nobody crazy yet, but the night was still young.

She stopped cold on her way back to the living room.

Brad and Rose were talking again. *Whispering.* Standing even closer than before.

Her stomach did somersaults, and as she was about to

walk away, Allison entered the hallway, arching a brow and offering Faye a sympathetic frown.

Faye shook her head. Brad wasn't Allison's first husband. And Rose was only a coworker … looking at her husband with hungry eyes.

Knees wobbling, Faye marched over to Brad. "I need your help with something. Now."

Allison gave her an approving nod.

Rose stiffened.

Faye pulled Brad to the stairway.

"What are you doing?" His expression was a brew of annoyance and confusion. "Rose thinks she has a few solid suspects."

"I think something's wrong with Hadley." Faye couldn't bring herself to admit her jealousy.

"Why? She seemed fine this morning."

"She doesn't want to come downstairs for the party."

"So? Football isn't her thing." Brad frowned. "I need to hear the rest of what Rose has to say. It would be good for you to hear, too."

"I—"

He took her hand and led her down the hall.

It was a relief that he wanted her there when he spoke with Rose, but she couldn't help thinking about Allison's first marriage. Or Jessica.

Something was definitely going on, even if it was just Brad's young coworker having a crush on him.

Faye would find a way to stop it in its tracks.

No matter what.

Chapter Fifteen

HADLEY FORCED a laugh at Larry Davis's joke as she finished a cookie shaped like a football helmet. She excused herself, then looked around for her parents. Mom was in a corner, talking with Allison, and Dad was laughing with some guy from work.

They weren't paying any attention to her. This was her chance to bolt.

After double-checking, she hurried upstairs and quickly changed into all black clothes, including a beanie. Once downstairs, she found her jacket with the most pockets — dark, of course — and tiptoed to the laundry room even though nobody would hear her over the party noise. It was part of the routine.

She opened the door to the backyard and covered the door cam with the same dark paper she used every time. She'd learned how to do it stealthily enough that it didn't register as movement. Regardless, it still made her nearly break out into a sweat.

Hadley ducked and crept underneath the window, careful not to be seen by any of the partygoers inside.

She felt her way across the rest of the house and to the fence, checking for the rock that used to always trip her up. She found the board with the knot, the one that had secretly been loosened to work as a door between the two yards.

She squeezed through, managing not to scratch herself, though it was a lot easier with a jacket covering so much of her. During the summer, she always ended up with scratches on her arms and legs. Luckily, her parents rarely noticed, and if they did, they seemed to buy even the flimsiest of her excuses.

It paid to be the responsible child. Zeke was such a screw-up, always getting in trouble at school and for the lamest things. Mom and Dad questioned nearly everything he did, even though she broke so many more rules.

Hadley pulled the boards back into place and hurried over to Duke's back door, pulling out her key and letting herself in. She drew in a deep breath, taking in the scent of his cologne.

Tears blurred her vision, and the lump in her throat grew big enough to explode.

"I'm going to hold it together."

She hurried upstairs, the reality of Duke's fate like an extra hundred pounds.

He was really gone. She could come over, but he wouldn't be here. Not any longer, and never again.

Pausing outside his bedroom, preparing herself to enter alone, the home's echo of silence like a constant taunting.

Tears spilled onto her face, but she didn't bother to wipe them away, letting them stream down her cheeks and drip onto her coat.

Duke's scent was stronger in here, the room where he once splashed his cologne.

It was so unfair. Why had someone killed *him*? What had he ever done to anybody?

He'd been the nicest person she'd ever met. Dad couldn't stand him but didn't really even have anything bad to say about him. He complained about their rivalries, sure. But never an ill word about his character. Duke loved helping people so much he'd turned it into a career, coaching people online and in person, sometimes for free, if he saw their potential.

He was the last person who should've been murdered.

She collapsed onto the bed and sobbed into his pillow, almost able to feel his comforting arm around her. Practically heard his whispers in her ear.

But none of it was real. Now all she had were photos and videos — she'd been playing those nonstop since getting home the night before. Her favorites were the ones of him laughing and telling her how much he loved her.

She'd never imagined how much she would appreciate those.

"Why, Duke? Did you fight back? Couldn't you have killed him instead of it being the other way around? What happened?"

Hadley looked at their string of texts for what had to be the five-hundredth time that day. Scrolled through pictures again. Played some videos.

It felt so good to hear his voice here, where it belonged. But it was so wrong with him gone. So wrong that she would never, ever see him again.

Hadley pulled the blankets close and cried out. Screamed into the bedding. Punched the mattress. Threw the pillows. Stomped.

Then went limp and buried herself under the covers again. Took in his cologne. It was everywhere. He was nowhere.

He didn't deserve it. Duke should've lived to be an old man.

Now he would be forever young. Immortalized at twenty-five.

After gasping for air, she looked at more photos but nearly dropped the phone. She'd already been here an hour. Her parents would realize she wasn't home. Mom was so insistent that she join the party. With any luck, the music blasting from her room would make Mom think she was studying and leave her alone.

But she needed to get home, regardless. She could always sneak back in after everyone went to bed — it wasn't like her parents ever suspected. Not as long as she was back before they woke up. Once, she had over-slept and needed to get ready for school here at Duke's. Then she'd had to sneak back home in the daylight. It'd been so nerve-wracking, she'd nearly puked.

But she pulled it off.

Hadley forced herself off the bed and found a sweat-shirt that had been tossed on his computer chair. The cotton still smelled like him. After pulling it on, she felt her way to the closet and found the gym bag tucked under some spare blankets.

She pulled out the papers. All the notes she wrote for him.

Relief washed through her. The police hadn't found them. Surely, they'd gone through his things searching for clues. If they'd checked the closet, they'd missed the bag.

Just as planned. Duke had adored her love letters, but they couldn't risk anyone else finding them. She'd been the one to insist he keep everything of hers hidden.

She would never have forgiven herself if he'd gotten in trouble. The laws were dumb. What was age, other than a number? Everything would've been fine once she turned eighteen.

They'd had less than a year until they could declare their love to the world.

Now they never would have the chance.

Hadley still couldn't tell a soul. She might become a suspect. People could claim she was a jilted lover, manufacturing some story about how Duke had broken up with her. It was ludicrous, but she wouldn't blame anyone for thinking that.

She'd think the same thing if she was on the outside looking in.

Slam!

Hadley froze. That sounded like one of the doors downstairs.

Nobody should be here. She and Duke had the only keys.

Had the cops come back for another look? Caution tape still surrounded the house.

They could arrest her for breaking in. But even if they didn't — Hadley did have a key — she would be a suspect. Or they might think Dad had a motive. There was no denying that if he knew about Hadley's relationship, he'd flip. Some might say he could go as far as killing. But he wouldn't.

Or would he?

She struggled to breathe. What if he did find out? Then what?

Would he murder Duke?

No. That was crazy. He'd be pissed, sure. Maybe even throw a few punches.

Voices sounded downstairs.

Hadley shoved the letters into her coat and put it back on. Cupped her ears, listening.

A man and a woman. Too far away to make out what they were saying.

She crept closer to the stairs.

Creak!

Hadley lifted her foot and silently cursed the floorboard.

The voices stopped.

She covered her mouth, her bladder threatening to give out.

Silence.

Hadley looked around for a place to hide. What she really needed was a way outside. But she was on the second floor. Her only escape was a leap through the window.

If only the apple tree was closer. Or the ground, like her house with its sloping yard. The drop was too far. Though if her choices were a broken leg or an arrest, or death if the people downstairs were the murderers, then she would deal with a cast.

Or she had too wild an imagination, and the people downstairs were neither cops nor criminals. Either way, she wasn't supposed to be there.

She needed to either get out unnoticed or wait this out.

And waiting could get her caught.

The voices started again.

Hadley exhaled and tiptoed toward the staircase, careful not to put much weight on any one floorboard.

It paid off. Not a sound.

She would definitely have to pee as soon as she returned home.

If she got there.

No. She *would*. This wasn't the time for drama.

Unless it was the perfect time.

Pulse drumming in her ears, she stepped onto the first

stair. She couldn't tell if it made noise or not. There was no time to waste worrying. She drew measured breaths, but heard only her heart.

Hadley continued down, her hearing slowly returning to normal. By the time she made it to the first floor, she could hear the pair of voices, though still too muffled to make out any words.

A man and a woman. That much was obvious.

They sounded close to the front entry.

Hadley could get to the back door without being seen.

Hopefully.

Thunk!

She froze.

Chink!

It sounded like they were trying to break something.

Anger festered in her chest. It wasn't bad enough that Duke was dead, but these people felt the need to break into his house and ruin his things?

She had to do something. But what? The intruders might have weapons, while she had only her love letters.

There were plenty of knives in the kitchen, and Duke had a gun upstairs. She didn't know what kind. But given all her practice at the range over the years with Dad and all the various weapons he had placed into her hands, Hadley could figure it out.

She bolted up the stairs.

Creak!

Her breath hitched. She pressed herself against the wall. Listened.

Voices, with no discernible words.

She was halfway up. Could go either way. Darted to the top. Ran around the corner. Tried to listen. Breathing too hard. Beads of sweat formed along her hairline.

Footsteps.

Hadley couldn't get to Duke's room without being seen from the bottom of the staircase.

The voices were closer. Whispering.

She still couldn't make out any words. Forced herself to take slow breaths. Cupped her ears, inched closer to the stairs.

"… someone here …"

"This way … impossible …"

Her mind raced. She couldn't get to the gun, but there had to be something else. Anything would do at this point. The bathroom was closest. Had to have something. A plunger? Razor blades? Throw mouthwash in their eyes?

"… knife … evidence."

Duke's killers. Coming back to the scene of the crime.

If they found her, they wouldn't hesitate to kill her, too. And if they'd overpowered her man, they would definitely be able to overtake her.

"Down … Brad."

Brad? As in, her father?

Or had she misheard that?

She must have. She was barely picking up anything they said.

The talking continued, but nothing made sense.

Except for her father's possible involvement. If Dad had discovered Duke and Hadley's relationship, he *could* be mad enough to kill. And crazy as that sounded, someone downstairs had said his name.

Her blood boiled. It made too much sense not to be true.

Footsteps crept away.

Away.

Her legs nearly gave out. They weren't heading her way.

A baseball bat. Duke had one in a spare bedroom. From his glory days in high school.

He'd understand if she needed to bloody it. It might be her only way out of the house alive.

She made it to the room without a sound. It was hard to see in the dark, even with her eyes adjusted. She felt her way, bumping into a dresser, and after her hand brushed a trophy, she found the bat on a shelf.

It teetered.

Her stomach plunged.

She grabbed it and steadied it. Bumped the bat.

It rolled toward the edge.

Her fingers brushed it. As it tumbled off the shelf.

She whispered for it to stop. Pleaded as she reached for it. Maneuvered herself under the bat to break its fall. Somehow managed to catch the thing between her side and arm. Wrapped her fingers around it and squeezed. Clung to the wood while desperately trying to catch her breath.

The gun would've been the better idea.

Or it could've been worse, given her current clumsiness.

She needed to get outside. It was dumb to think she could face off with two people. And it wasn't like Duke could use any of his stuff anymore. But that didn't give them the right to come in and ruin any of it.

He also wouldn't want her risking her life over some things.

Slam!

Were they leaving? Or was it a trick? They could be trying to lure her out.

She hurried to the stairs, gripping her new weapon.

Silence.

Hadley waited a moment before making her way down again. This time, she avoided any creaky boards.

At the bottom, she listened. Then, breath hitched, headed toward the front door. She was ready to clobber someone, despite her shaking hands. Or at least give it her best effort. Looked around. Didn't see the burglars or what they had been destroying.

Hadley darted to the window.

Two people, a man and a woman. Racing away.

Heading up the walkway to her house.

Probably for a conversation with Dad.

Chapter Sixteen

FAYE WAVED goodbye to her client and headed back to her station to sweep the hair from underneath the chair.

Cheryl stepped in front of her as she was reaching for the broom. "I heard about Duke. What a shock!"

"I know." She moved around her friend and swept the mess, trying to ignore the pressure building near her temples.

"He lived near you, right?"

"Next door."

Cheryl gasped. "Did it happen there?"

Mandy and Bella inched closer.

Faye sighed. May as well share the story now, while none of them had clients to hear. "Yes."

"Were you guys home?" Bella asked.

"Your kids?" Mandy asked.

Faye considered her words carefully. "The police don't know exactly when it happened, so it's hard to say."

Cheryl embraced her. "You must be so shaken up! I don't think I could come into work after one of my clients was murdered so close to home."

"I've had the weekend to process it. Besides, the neighborhood Super Bowl party was held in his honor."

"It's so nice everyone could come together like that."

Faye smiled and checked the time. "It was, but I've got to get ready for my next client."

"Are you sure you're okay?" Bella's doe eyes were even bigger than usual. "I'd seriously be freaking out. I mean, he's one of your regulars."

"And super hot," Mandy added.

Bella shoved her. "Not the time. Seriously?"

"Duke was a really nice guy." Faye sprayed the chair and wiped it. "He was the kind of guy that would give anyone the shirt off his back. I think that's what's the hardest. It doesn't make sense why someone would want him dead."

Mandy leaned closer. "Did he give you any clues?"

"What do you mean?"

"He was in every week, and you two were always chatting. He ever say anything about someone who didn't like him?"

"It was every *other* week. And no, he mostly talked about things that were going well for him. His business always seemed to be booming. He'd just hired another virtual assistant because it was too much for him, even with the two he already had."

The other stylists exchanged knowing looks.

"What?"

Bella tilted her head. "It sounds like you know a lot about him."

"Not really." Faye glanced toward the door. No client coming to save her.

"Do the police know about his assistants?"

Faye tidied her supplies. "I don't know. They're more interested in asking questions than confiding in me."

Ding!

A customer walked inside.

Saved by the bell.

Mandy patted Faye's shoulder. "Think about what he told you. There's probably a clue in there somewhere. Even if it was just a passing comment."

Faye didn't respond as the others dispersed to their stations. Her mind turned over their recent conversations. She'd already replayed them what felt like hundreds of times, but maybe being at work, where she'd spent the most time cutting his hair, would jog a memory.

The rest of the morning went by in a blaze and she distracted herself by asking her clients about their weekends and telling them about Hadley's lead role in the play. None of them brought up Duke. Though between clients, she did think back to their conversations with him in her chair.

As she was sweeping purple curls, something Duke said about a month ago struck her. He'd been complaining about an online troll who refused to leave him alone.

After the last client left the salon before lunch, her coworkers crowded around her again.

"Think of anything?" Mandy asked.

Faye hesitated.

"You did!" Bella's eyes lit up. "Tell us everything."

"It's probably nothing."

"It's definitely something." Cheryl stepped closer.

They all stared.

"He had an online troll. But he sounded annoyed about it, not worried."

"Because the troll was threatening him?" Bella plopped onto Faye's chair. "Did he want Duke dead?"

"He didn't say anything about death threats." She

focused, trying to recall what exactly he'd said. "It was a few weeks ago. He could've already resolved it."

Mandy pursed her lips. "Or the situation could have escalated."

"Have you told the cops?" Cheryl asked. "That could be a clue."

"I just remembered."

"You *have* to tell them," Mandy urged.

The others nodded in agreement.

"I'll think about it." Faye marched to the back room and pulled her sack lunch from the fridge.

"*Think* about it?" Bella exclaimed. "A great guy was murdered, and you have a clue that could solve the case."

"Or it could be nothing." Faye sat at the table and dug into her jalapeño popper chicken salad. "There's a huge jump from internet troll to cold-blooded killer."

Mandy sat, holding Faye's gaze. "Or maybe there isn't."

"The police have spent the weekend at his place — it's still taped off. I'm sure they've pulled everything from his computer and phone. I wouldn't be telling them anything they don't already have access to."

"But you don't *know* that."

Faye's stomach churned acid, and she put the lid back on her salad. "Maybe."

"No maybe about it."

She drew in a deep breath.

Cheryl rested her hand on Faye's. "Are you okay, sweetie?"

"Brad doesn't know I've been cutting Duke's hair."

"So?" Mandy asked. "My partner doesn't know about most of my clients."

"Are any of your clients your partner's neighborhood rival?"

All three scooted closer, showing surprise in their own ways.

"Duke was Brad's nemesis?" Bella asked.

"It was nothing serious," Faye said quickly. "Nemesis is an awfully big word for their friendly competitions. Super Bowl decorations, Christmas lights, fireworks displays. That sort of thing."

"Is he a suspect?" Mandy asked, then left her mouth hanging open.

"No. The police have only asked us questions."

Bella said, "Brad can't seriously be that upset. I mean, the guy is dead. And it's only hair."

"You don't get it. I know it sounds crazy, but he really didn't want us interacting with Duke. The guy really got under his skin."

"Wait." Mandy narrowed her eyes. "You said he and Duke had a friendly rivalry, now you're saying he didn't want any of you interacting with him. Which is it?"

"A friendly rivalry." Her stomach knotted, but she managed a smile.

"Why didn't he want you interacting?" Bella asked.

"It got under his skin."

"So, he and Duke *weren't* friends?" Cheryl asked.

"The competition was friendly. That doesn't mean they were buddies."

Mandy lifted a brow. "Sounds suspicious to me."

Faye never should've said anything. "You're making it sound worse than it was."

"Really?" Bella looked at her. "Your husband didn't want you interacting with Duke, and you don't want him to know you were cutting Duke's hair. Sounds pretty cut and dried to me."

Cheryl frowned. "I didn't realize Brad was like that."

"He's not. Everyone has their quirks. That's one of his. I'm telling you, it's no big deal."

"Why didn't you ever mention it before?" Mandy asked.

"Do you have other rules you have to live by to keep him happy?" Bella asked.

Faye pinched the bridge of her nose. "No."

"Do you feel safe at home?" Cheryl asked.

"Oh my gosh!" Faye leaped up, nearly knocking the plastic chair over. "I'm not an abused wife! It's just one little secret — every marriage has them. This only seems like a big deal because Duke is now dead. Maybe I'll tell the cops, and maybe I won't. But I really don't think the troll issue has anything to do with the murder."

She shoved her salad back in the fridge before storming into the salon. Another fifteen minutes before her next client.

Footsteps sounded behind her on the tile.

Faye rushed outside and stood under the eaves, watching the rain pour down. But it didn't soothe her frayed nerves. Now her coworkers thought Brad was some kind of control freak or an abusive husband — exactly what she *didn't* want them thinking.

Unfortunately, given their recent argument about a home salon, standing up for her husband wasn't as easy as she wanted it to be.

After a few deep breaths, she began to relax.

Could the other stylists be right? If she told the detective about the online troll, it might move the focus away from Brad. That would definitely be in their favor. Especially if it panned out as a legitimate lead.

But if word got back around to Brad that Faye had been the one to tell them, that would surely invite a new set of problems into their marriage. They'd need to return to counseling. No doubt about that.

Though really, that might not be a bad idea. Both Hadley and Zeke were upset about the murder. Something like that would've shaken her up at their ages. It shook her even now at her current age. She was worried about her children's safety and preoccupied with her little secret. And that's *all* it was, nothing to worry about. Her coworkers were making far too big a deal about nothing.

Maybe Faye could find a way to mention the internet troll to the detective in a way that wouldn't add more suspicion than there already was. She'd already screwed that up with the other stylists.

She'd have to be far more careful when speaking with the detective. This was a practice session. Something to learn from so she didn't ruin anything with the investigation.

But word might get back to Brad. The detective would want to know when Duke told her about the troll. She could *not* say work. What if the cops put two and two together, figuring out that she'd trimmed his hair that night, even without her saying a word?

She flashed back to seeing the blood behind Brad's ear the night of the murder.

What had he really been doing? Was it really something innocent?

And what about the way Rose had been hanging on Brad at the party?

He was hiding something.

Faye needed to find out what.

Chapter Seventeen

BRAD KILLED the engine but didn't get out of the car. His head pounded, and the only thing he wanted was to go upstairs and sleep. Kurt still hadn't shown up to work nor given Brad any of the promised help — no call from an attorney or from the man himself. His boss might have been nursing a hangover from his party the night before — it wouldn't be the first time he'd missed work for that — but it was inexcusable for him to leave Brad hanging like that for this long. Kurt had promised to help him on Saturday morning, and it was now Monday evening.

To make matters worse, the detective had shown up at work asking questions. Based on what she was asking, they had nothing new on Brad. She just wanted to intimidate him by appearing at his job and even tossed a few queries at the other employees. Rose had jumped to Brad's defense, saying she and Justin had seen Brad and Faye that night, to which Justin agreed. But Rose stood so close to Brad and acted so flirtatious, she almost made it seem like *they* had something to hide.

The girl had never been the brightest on a personal

level, though it could've been an act since she was such a talented assassin, or maybe she had some small crush on Brad, but either way, she wasn't helping his case. She'd piqued the detective's interest, which would only make things harder on Brad.

Before Detective Stewart had left, Brad mentioned Lucas saying that Fallon and Duke had had an altercation. She made a note but hadn't seemed all that interested in following the lead. Probably thought Brad was making it up.

He dug into the glove box, found a bottle of ibuprofen, and popped a few, swallowing them with a flat soda. With any luck, they would get him through dinner, and then he could either go to sleep or lock himself in his office and try to reach Kurt. Again.

He took a few deep breaths and prepared himself for his family. As upset as everyone was about Duke, they'd likely all be mopey. He needed to help them focus on the positive so they could all move on with their lives.

He stepped inside and heard cartoons and Luna's laughter from the living room. The scent of something cooking made him salivate. Roast?

His evening was turning around.

Until he entered the kitchen. As Faye mixed something in a bowl at the counter, Allison stirred something in a pot on the stove.

Brad bit back an annoyed retort and instead kissed Faye, ignoring her guest. "Need any help with dinner?"

"No. But can you check on Zeke? He's supposed to be doing homework, but I think he's still playing Zombie Wars."

"You bet." Then he whispered in her ear. "She isn't staying for dinner, is she?"

Faye shook her head and gave him one of her looks, which meant they would talk later.

Yes, they would.

Brad snuggled Luna before checking on Zeke, who was glued to his computer and tapped his shoulder.

His son looked up, guilt in his eyes, and pulled off his headphones. "This round is almost over. Then I'm going to start my algebra homework. I swear."

"Your mom said you were already supposed to be doing that."

"This round went long." He eyed the screen. "And my squad is winning. Please let me finish. I'll wash the dinner dishes. For the rest of the week."

"All right. But you better finish all of your homework."

"Thanks, Dad!" Zeke beamed as he pulled back on his headset and spoke to his online friends while adjusting the mic.

At least he was on someone's good side for a change.

Brad patted his son's shoulder before changing into something more comfortable, then checking his phone for a call from Kurt. And, of course, *still nothing*.

He glanced out the window before heading back downstairs.

Allison was walking down the sidewalk. Brad swore he heard a choir of angels.

He hurried downstairs and stirred creamed corn as Faye checked the temperature of the roast. "Why is Allison around so much suddenly?"

"She's just being friendly."

"Friendly?"

"Is there an echo in here?"

He stepped back as she pulled the meat out of the oven. "You don't really think she has any other motive?"

"I called her to come and get her decorations if you

must know. I didn't want them to get mixed up with our things and potentially lost."

"She doesn't like me."

"Perhaps you should try being a little more likable."

His skin prickled. "You're putting this on me? The woman has never had a good thing to say about me or any of my decorations. Nothing is *ever* good enough for her."

"Maybe she's lonely. Or she's worried about us since the murder was so close to our family."

"Or she wants all the dirt. We're the ones most likely to know what's going on since the police won't leave us alone."

"Did the detective show up at your work, too?"

Brad gave her a double-take. "She showed up at the salon?"

"Yes."

"What did you tell her?"

"Same thing we've been saying. If she's waiting for us to change our story, she'll be waiting a while. What did she ask you?"

"Nothing new. That woman just wants to get under our skin."

"Or she wants to solve the case," Faye said on her way to the table. "As much as she may want us to be guilty, it doesn't matter. We didn't do anything. Right?"

"What do you mean by that?"

She put her roast on the table and held his gaze. "If neither of us committed the murder, we don't have anything to worry about."

"Not that. You said 'right.' You don't believe me?"

"That isn't what I said."

"What did you mean by *right*?"

They stared each other down.

He stepped closer, his pulse spiking. "Do you think I did something to our neighbor?"

"Why was there blood behind your ear that night?"

"I already told you. A guy cut himself at the convention."

"And it got behind your ear?"

"Yes. Some people are total idiots. And you'd be surprised how many of them show up at knife shows. They should require an IQ test with entry."

She frowned.

"You don't believe me?"

He opened his mouth to repeat the lie, but Luna bounced into the room. "Dinner ready?"

"Yes." Faye gave her a sweet smile. "Can you get your brother and sister, please?"

"Okay, Mommy." She skipped into the hall.

"Will you set the table?" Faye asked him, buzzing about the room, not giving him an opportunity to continue the conversation.

A few minutes later, everyone sat, filling their plates. Hadley barely put anything on hers. Must've been on another one of her diets. Zeke piled on enough for the both of them. Faye ate, avoiding Brad's gaze.

All because of Allison's visit. Who knew what drivel she'd been feeding Faye? Poisoning her against him?

Brad sighed, his appetite waning before he took his first bite.

"Did anyone see the ads for the new 80s show starting soon?" Zeke grinned. "It looks like a cross between *Jaws* and *Breakfast Club*. Gonna be totally awesome."

"Can I watch it?" Luna asked.

"Not if it's like *Jaws*," Faye said.

She pouted.

"Sounds lame, anyway." Hadley rolled her eyes dramatically at Zeke.

Brad turned to her. "Be nice to your brother."

Hadley slammed her palm on the table. "You're always siding with him!"

"You need to relax."

"Relax?" Her face flushed. "Are you kidding me? He's an 80s-obsessed nerd that everyone makes fun of. You should be encouraging him to do things to fit in."

Zeke glared at her. "You're just worried I'll embarrass you."

"Worried? You *already* humiliated me. Do you know what it's like being your sister?"

"Thankfully, no." He inhaled his corn.

"Kids," Brad warned.

"This is ridiculous! I'm done." Hadley rose and snatched her plate so quickly that her roast nearly rolled off. She turned to Brad, her face reddening. "And I'm totally sick of you!"

"You need to watch your tone."

"You're clueless!" She put her plate back down and stormed away.

Brad leaped up.

Faye stopped him. "Let her calm down."

Zeke piled more roast on his plate. "Don't take it personally, Dad. She's been pissy ever since the weekend. I can't even look at her without her insulting me."

"I'll talk to her."

"Or," Faye said, "we should try *listening* to her."

"Listening? She—"

"There's that echo again."

Brad gritted his teeth. "As long as she's living under our roof, she needs to follow our rules."

"Something is obviously upsetting her. She'll be more likely to open up if we aren't heavy-handed."

"She's right." Luna nodded enthusiastically. "Girls just want to be heard."

Brad and Faye exchanged a curious glance.

A few minutes later, Zeke gathered the dishes. "I'm washing all the dishes. You guys go *listen* to Hadley."

Luna went back to her cartoons while Brad and Faye headed upstairs.

"I'm really worried about her," she said, stopping them with a whisper in front of Hadley's room.

"It's called being a teenager. We gave our parents the same snark, remember?"

Faye didn't look convinced.

"You don't remember?"

"I do, but this is so unlike her — to be *that* rude to you and Zeke. Something is obviously bothering her."

"Probably boy troubles."

She wrung her hands. "But she hasn't talked about a boyfriend."

"Because she would tell us everything, right?"

"She *has* always kept me in the loop. You freak out about boys, so she doesn't tell you anything anymore."

"That was one time, and the kid was nothing but trouble."

"One time is all it takes."

He'd had enough. "Why don't *you* listen to what she has to say. I always get everything wrong."

"That isn't what I said!"

"You didn't have to."

"Would you stop making this about you and focus on our daughter? She needs us."

"*About me?* Is that what you think I'm doing?"

"I know that's what you're doing."

"Okay, then. You listen to Hadley. I need to talk to Kurt."

Her brows drew together. "You didn't speak with him at work?"

"He's ghosting me, despite knowing the police keep questioning me."

"Can't we find our own lawyer? Why do we need his?"

Brad drew in a deep breath, considered his wording. "He has access to the best attorneys, and we won't have to pay full price for their services."

"Makes sense, but a decent lawyer is better than none, which is all we have right—"

"I *know*. That's why I need to get a hold of him."

She nodded. "Okay. Let's divide and conquer. I'll find out what's bothering Hadley, and you call Kurt."

Finally, they were on the same page.

But the look in her eyes told him that she had more to say and maybe even wanted to say it.

Brad would have to deal with that later.

Chapter Eighteen

FAYE KISSED LUNA. "Five more minutes, then you have to get up."

"Thanks, Mommy." She rolled over, pulled the blanket over her head.

Faye smiled, remembering when Hadley had been that young. Ten years felt like a few minutes. If only there was a way to slow time and keep them little forever.

She pushed the nostalgia away and went into the hall. The shower started in the main bathroom. That meant either Hadley or Zeke. Probably Hadley, but given how mopey and closed off she'd been the last few days, she could be the one still in bed.

Faye gave a light knock on Hadley's door, waited, then pushed it open. The room was dim, and the bed already made. Some of her heaviness lifted. Maybe Hadley was pushing past whatever she was going through. Might be hormones. That made a lot of sense, given the timeframe.

She started to close the door but stopped at the sight of a midnight blue sweatshirt draped over her daughter's chair. Duke's company logo was embroidered across the front.

He'd worn the same shirt when getting his haircut a few times.

What was Hadley doing with it?

Had he loaned it to her? It was like she'd told the other stylists, he was the type of guy to give someone the shirt off his back. Maybe Hadley had been cold, and he'd given that to her.

But they lived next door. If Hadley needed a sweater, she could've come inside to grab something of her own.

Faye stumbled across the room and picked up the sweatshirt with shaking hands.

It smelled like cologne. Really, it smelled like Duke. Every time he sat in her salon chair, she got a whiff of his signature scent.

Her mind raced, desperately wanting to think of a scenario where the things she was thinking weren't entirely crazy.

She came up blank.

The shower stopped.

Faye hurried out of the room, barely remembering to pull Luna from bed. On her way to her bedroom, she knocked on Zeke's door.

"I'm up!"

"Just checking." She wasn't sure the words ever left her mouth.

Brad was gelling his hair in their room. Two gazes met in the mirror. "You okay?"

Faye shook her head. "You'll never believe what I just saw in Hadley's room."

"Another wolf spider?"

"Duke's sweatshirt."

"His sweatshirt?" Brad repeated. "You sure?"

"It has his company logo."

"Do you know how many people he's gotten to sell that MLM in this neighborhood?" Brad shook his head. "More than half the families at that party are in on it."

"But it smells like cologne."

Brad turned back to the mirror and studied his hair. "Probably some kid from school. Did you ask her about it?"

"She's in the shower."

"I'm sure it's no big deal."

"It smells like *his* cologne!"

He whipped around, his eyebrows furrowed. "And how do you know that?"

"He wore a lot of it. A unique scent. Made me think of our trip to Hawaii."

"In other words, it was flowery."

"Like the ocean. But that isn't the point. I'm worried about our daughter, Brad."

"Because she's seeing some kid who smells like the ocean? Sure, I can talk to her about finding a manlier boyfriend."

"I'm serious."

"So am I. But Hadley would never be involved with a guy like Duke."

"And what kind of a guy is that?"

"Besides being much too old for her, Duke was a predator."

"Predator?"

Brad nodded. "How else does someone become one of the highest-ranked sellers in an MLM company? Ninety percent of people who join those schemes never advance."

"Ninety percent?"

"Now, who has the echo? I made that number up, but you know what I'm saying. How many have you tried?

There was the makeup one, the vitamins, the oils, the candles—"

"Point taken." She scowled at him.

"I'll ask her about the shirt at breakfast. She'll say it belongs to some kid from the play. Watch."

"I hope you're right."

"Of course I am." Brad brightened, apparently struck by an idea. "There's an angle the detective might want to take. Someone could be pissed that Duke promised them the world, and they got stuck with a garage full of protein shakes. There's motive."

"To kill?"

"If somebody lost money, you'd better believe it."

"Maybe. But that still doesn't explain the shirt in Hadley's room smelling like Duke's cologne."

Brad crossed his arms. "What I want to know is why you're so convinced it's his. How close were you to him?"

"Not very."

"You sound defensive. Should I be worried?" His mouth formed a straight line.

"No!" Her stomach twisted, knowing he wouldn't be much happier learning that it hadn't been just one emergency haircut, that Duke had been one of her regulars. "It's expensive and stands out. That's all. He was a *kid*. Twenty-five or something? I could be his mom."

"An attractive mom. I wouldn't put it past him to—"

"I've heard enough. There was never *anything* between me and him. Ever." She glanced at the wall clock. "If I don't get to the kitchen, we're all going without breakfast this morning."

She called for the kids to hurry as she headed for the stairs. Scrambled eggs this morning. She liked sending everyone off with a robust meal in their bellies, so they wouldn't have to deal with being hungry all morning.

She'd been left to fend for herself as a kid too often and refused to let her kids live like that.

The things Brad said ran through her mind as she whisked the eggs and poured them into the hot nonstick pan. Could Duke have gone after Hadley romantically? *She* was a beautiful young woman. Many a teenage boy had given himself whiplash while trying to get a second look at her. So had college guys. Duke hadn't been much older than a college graduate.

It wasn't out of the realm of possibility.

But Duke? There wasn't a nicer guy around. He wouldn't prey on a teenager.

Or would he?

No. That would have been nuts. He couldn't have been bold enough to sit in Faye's chair every other week if he was seeing her daughter.

Unless he was trying to distract her, to make her think better of him than he was.

He *could* have been playing her.

Her stomach churned acid.

Black smoke flew up from the eggs.

She pulled the pan away from the burner and stirred, shaking at the thought of her neighbor being a child predator. He was no kid. At twenty-five, he was a man.

And his sweatshirt was in her daughter's room. There was no question it was his. No high schooler would wear that expensive cologne. Or the shirt. Kids would make fun of any of their peers involved in an MLM.

She picked the burned bits out of the eggs, her mind racing. What if Duke had made an advance on Hadley? She could've fought back. Threatened to turn him in. How would he have responded? If he turned around and threatened her back, how might Hadley have reacted?

Her blood ran cold.

What if her daughter killed him to keep him from harassing her — or worse?

That would be a motive.

Those detectives could be looking at the wrong member of the Morris family.

She needed to get to the bottom of this as soon as possible. But how could she get her daughter to open up about something so serious?

The kids trickled down for breakfast, and Faye handed them each a plate. She made light conversation about homework and after-school activities, but she watched Hadley pick at her food. She'd used heavy makeup under her eyes — to hide the dark circles, no doubt. Her eyes were slightly bloodshot, cast down at the table. No teasing her brother this morning.

Something was definitely off.

Did Duke hurt Hadley? Had she been forced to kill him?

Faye had to ask. Look for nonverbal signs which would speak louder than her words.

This wasn't a conversation she could have with Zeke and Luna present.

But it also couldn't wait.

Chapter Nineteen

BRAD SAT with his eggs at the quiet table. Hadley pushed her food around her plate while Zeke ate like he was starving. Faye paced the room, glancing at their eldest every three seconds.

After a few bites, Brad cleared his throat and looked at Hadley. "Did you join an MLM and not tell us?"

"What?"

"That hoodie in your room."

Her face paled. "It's not like that."

"What, then?"

"It … It's my boyfriend's."

He scratched his chin. "Since when do you have a boyfriend?"

"Ugh, really?"

"I'm serious."

Faye inched closer to the table, her hands wringing together.

Hadley looked at her. "Mom, help me out."

"I'm not sure who your boyfriend is, either."

"Maverick. Ring any bells?"

Brad tried to remember. It sounded vaguely familiar. "From your play?"

She shook her head. "You were reading my private texts."

"Are you talking about the texts that showed up on your screen when you left your phone in the middle of the living room?"

"Yes." She glared at him. "Those were private."

"Not when we pay for the phone."

"As I explained to you then, Maverick is my boyfriend. I have to get to school before I'm late." She hurried out of the room without another word.

Brad exchanged a concerned glance with Faye.

Zeke scooted back. "You're seriously going to let her get away with not putting her plate away two meals in a row? If I start acting like her, can I do that, too?"

Brad gave him a warning glance.

"Fine." Zeke tossed his plate into the sink with more force than necessary and stomped up the stairs.

"Why's everyone in a bad mood?" Luna asked.

"Because they're teenagers." Brad rose and put his dishes away.

Faye caught up with him as he was heading to his office. "Do you believe Hadley?"

"About Derrick?"

"Maverick."

"Whatever. It's such a pretentious name. But it's just like I told you — she's seeing some kid from school. And I apparently already knew about him. I suppose you're going to tell me I'm parent of the year."

"I'm worried about her." Faye grabbed his arm.

"Teenage girls are moody. I'd be worried if she *wasn't* being difficult."

"What if she's hiding something?"

Brad glanced at his watch. "Like what?"

"That sweatshirt is Duke's." She looked around and lowered her voice. "What if something happened, and she killed him?"

The words felt like a punch to the throat. "What?"

"Think about it."

"She told us the shirt doesn't belong to Duke."

"And you believe her?"

"It's Maverick's sweatshirt. Why would she have Duke's when she has a boyfriend?"

Faye's eyes narrowed. "She's lying about Maverick. If Duke hurt her—"

"I'd have killed him myself." Anger surged through him.

"Don't say that around anyone else!"

"Obviously. You're making too much of the shirt. Our little girl wouldn't get involved with that loser. I made it clear that I didn't want any of us talking to him."

"And teenagers are *so* good following parental direction."

Brad took several measured breaths. The thought of Duke even looking at his daughter was enough to boil his blood. The thought of that man-child's hands on her made him want to put his fist through a wall. Or Duke's face, but it was too late for that.

Faye pressed her palms on his chest. "What if she killed him?"

"She's no killer."

And he knew killers. His little girl didn't have it in her. She was feisty, but that was as far as it went.

Tears shone in Faye's eyes. "If he was pressuring her—"

"She wouldn't have his shirt hanging on her chair!

Think about it: Hadley would have burned the damned thing if she'd killed him."

Faye stepped back. "You do have a point."

"Precisely. Instead of worrying about our dead neighbor, we need to find out what we can about this Maverick punk. I need to meet my daughter's boyfriend and give him the dad talk."

"You really don't think she was involved with Duke?"

"No. But do you know what does concern me?"

Faye shook her head.

"Your *certainty* that the sweatshirt belonged to Duke."

She straightened her stance. "It has his company logo — which everyone on the street knows — and his cologne is unique. Nothing strange about that."

"Isn't there?"

"How can you suggest such a thing?"

"Because my wife seems to know an awful lot about our next door neighbor. I see the way women look at him. Some men, too."

Faye sighed. "You're being ridiculous."

"Am I?"

"Of course you are."

Faye put her hands on her hips. "If anyone should be suspicious, it's me."

"You?" He struggled to keep his temper under control. "What do you mean?"

"Rose."

He stared at her in disbelief. "Really?"

"Yes. She was hanging all over you at the party."

Brad couldn't deny that, but he needed to in order to prove the truth — that nothing was going on between them. "We were just talking. She was telling me what she'd learned from questioning the neighbors. Which really wasn't much, by the way. Not a single thing I could give to the cops."

"People thought you two looked cozy."

"Who?" he demanded.

"Allison said—"

Brad pulled on his hair. "Allison. Of course! That woman has it out for me, just like I've been telling you since she started coming around. Do you think she'd be so friendly to you if Duke hadn't died next door? She wants gossip, Faye. She doesn't care about you."

Her nostrils flared. "You're jealous that I have a friend. I've been leaning on you for so long, now you have competition."

"Would you listen to yourself?"

"Stop deflecting! People noticed how close you and Rose were the other night."

"I can't believe you'd even think that."

"Really? What about Jessica?"

He stumbled back. "We moved past that a decade ago."

"So, I'm just supposed to *forget*?"

"That *was* our agreement."

Fire burned in her expression. "I can forgive, but I can't forget. Not when I see you so close to someone who looks like Rose. It brings everything flooding back."

He counted silently to ten. "Nothing happened with Jessica. Not even a kiss. Do you happen to remember that?"

"Dr. Trellis called it an emotional affair. That's not nothing."

"That shrink blew it way out of proportion. Even so, we managed to move on."

"Have we, really? You're not close to Rose?"

"Not remotely." He laced his fingers through hers and

held her gaze. "You're the only woman for me, Faye. We've had our ups and downs — sometimes it seems like more downs than ups — but we're meant for one another. I wouldn't do anything to jeopardize that. Especially not after Jessica. You have to believe me."

Faye's expression softened. "The same holds true for me. There was *nothing* going on between me and Duke. Ever. It's only ever been you."

The look in her eyes told him more than her words had. It was all true. His stance relaxed. "Nothing has changed. We're all good."

One side of her mouth curved down slightly. "I think we should see Dr. Trellis again."

A bolt of rage surged through him, but showing it would only reinforce Faye's suspicion, so he pushed it down. "Neither of us accused. We questioned. Nothing wrong with that. An unhealthy couple wouldn't be able to do that."

"Don't you remember how much she helped us last time? With your anger and dealing with your dad's death."

"There's a huge difference between needing help to get past my dad's murder and having a neighbor killed that none of us knew." He glanced at the time. "We're both going to be late if we don't get going. How about we think on this and talk tonight?"

Her eyes lit up. "You'll consider it?"

He gave a slight nod. "We'll talk later."

She squeezed him before heading down the stairs. "I'm so glad to hear it."

Brad buried his face in his palms. Now on top of everything else he had to deal with, he had to figure out how to convince his wife that the family didn't need a shrink.

Chapter Twenty

HADLEY DUCKED behind the kid in front of her to hide another yawn. She'd barely gotten four hours of sleep. Then her parents freaking out on her at breakfast — exhausting.

Life would be so much easier if she could tell them what she was really dealing with — a dead boyfriend instead of some stupid made-up one. She needed to find a way to lock her bedroom door to keep Mom and Dad out. She'd never imagined they'd notice the sweatshirt.

"Hadley." The teacher's sharp tone pulled her from her thoughts.

"What?"

Mrs. Johnston pointed to the speaker. "You're needed at the office."

Several kids snickered and a few made comments about her being in trouble.

Hadley faked a laugh as she stuffed her things into the bag and marched into the hallway. She could be in trouble for all she knew, especially considering how poorly she'd been doing in her classes all week. Maybe this was about her history quiz. She'd bombed that for sure.

What if they weren't going to let her try out for the next school play? Her heart sank at the thought. She would beg and plead, even offer to do janitorial work. Whatever it took.

When she got to the office, the secretary pointed her to a room. At least it wasn't the principal's office. But there was no nameplate on the door, so she didn't know who was on the other side.

She rapped quickly.

"Come in."

Her stomach knotted, but she stood tall and held her head high as she entered.

The detective who had come to the play. She sat beside a different cop.

"Thank you for coming, Hadley," she said. "Have a seat."

It wasn't like she had a choice.

Once seated, the detective reintroduced herself and Officer Lang — he looked almost as young as Hadley.

She nodded and waited. Did they know she'd been in Duke's house the other night? Or had they figured out she was dating him? What if they thought she had killed him? Or were they still looking at Dad?

The silence seemed to creep forever, the second hand on the clock moving in slow motion. "What can I help you with?"

"We're here about the death of Duke Hill," said Officer Lang.

"That's what I figured." She squeezed her hands together under the table where they couldn't see. "What can I do?"

Detective Stewart paused before answering. "Tell us about your relationship with the deceased."

An icy chill smothered her. They knew. "What do you mean?"

Officer Lang leaned forward. "You knew him well enough to be texting him late at night."

Hadley's breath hitched. Was that all they had? Texts? Her mind raced to their cover story. "He was tutoring me."

Detective Stewart scribbled a note. "Do you text all of your tutors after eleven?"

"I hadn't heard from him," she said quickly. "I was worried he might not be able to help me before the Super Bowl."

"Help you?"

"With my singing."

The two exchanged an unreadable expression.

Her heart sank.

Detective Stewart turned back to her. "He tutored you in singing?"

Hadley nodded. Hopefully, they couldn't see the beads of sweat forming around her forehead.

"I wasn't aware he was a singer."

She cleared her throat. "He used to coach his sister when they were growing up. When he heard me singing, practicing for my play, he offered to help."

"Explain."

"I was in my backyard singing some lines for my play. There was one song, in particular, tripping me up. He popped his head over the fence and offered me a tip. I didn't really get what he meant since I hadn't had any formal lessons, so he said he could tutor me."

They exchanged another look.

Officer Lang rubbed his chin. "There's one thing that doesn't make sense to me."

"What?" Hadley's heart hammered.

"Why were you so desperate to talk to your tutor *after* your play was done? His phone showed half a dozen texts from you."

The room shrunk around her. "I, uh … he was supposed to go to one of my shows. I wanted to know what he thought of my performance."

"It couldn't have waited until the next day?"

She shrugged. "I guess."

"But you wanted to know right then? It was too hard to wait?" offered Lang.

"Exactly."

The detective scrawled more notes. "Did the deceased help you with anything else?"

Hadley didn't like the way she said the word *help*. "I don't know what you mean."

"Math? PE? Science?"

"No."

"You two texted a lot, didn't you?"

"I don't know."

"You don't *know*?" Officer Lang stared her down.

"Not more than my friends."

"So, Duke was a friend?"

"He was my tutor."

"Do kids usually text their tutors as much as you texted Duke?"

"How would I know?" Irritation rippled through her. "And how is this helping to find the murderer?"

"We'll ask the questions," said the detective.

She glanced at the clock again. The bell would ring soon. She'd use that as her excuse to get out of there.

Officer Lang scooted closer to Hadley. "Did Duke have nicknames for all the girls he tutored?"

"What do you mean?"

"Your texts were under *Angel Eyes*."

"He, uh, it was just like you said — a nickname."

"Seems like an awfully personal nickname for a tutor."

"It was nice. That's all."

"You sure?"

She pulled her gaze from his. "Yeah. Can I go now?"

"We have a few more questions."

Hadley glared at him. "I'm missing an important lecture."

"We're almost done." The detective gave her a plastic smile. "Do you know of anyone who didn't like Duke?"

"Why would I? It wasn't like I hung out with him and his friends."

"Didn't you?"

"No."

The room was silent so long, she was sure they would finally let her go.

"Did he mention anyone to you?" asked the detective.

"He didn't."

"Are you sure? Maybe you should think about it for a moment."

Heat crept into her cheeks as she pretended to think. "He never said anything to me about that."

"You were his neighbor. Did you see or hear anything suspicious?"

"I'd tell you if I knew anything that would help. I want whoever killed him to go to jail!"

Another glance exchanged.

Hadley pushed her chair back. "I need to get back to class."

"We have just a few more questions, then you can go."

"Fine."

"Where were you on Friday night between your first and second showing of the play?"

"Wh-what?" Hadley's mouth went entirely dry.

Detective Stewart tapped the table. "None of your friends recall seeing you for an entire hour. Everyone was eating and getting ready. You weren't there."

"Yes, I was."

The detective's expression darkened.

Hadley's hands shook. She hadn't thought anyone noticed her absence.

Everyone had.

Duke had brought her a boxed meal from their favorite restaurant. And flowers. He'd even gotten his hair cut for her. He couldn't wait to spend time with her later to celebrate a job well done.

But he'd never responded to her texts.

"Ms. Morris?"

She sat up taller. "I don't know why nobody remembers me being there. Maybe they were too busy with their own preparations. I know I was."

"Where were you during that hour?" said Lang.

"I was there!" Hadley refused to let the cops see her crying. But desperation clawed at her. She had to think of something to change the topic. Anything other than this.

"And you—?"

"There were two people at his house Sunday night!"

"What?" The detective was visibly shaken.

"Yeah. I saw them."

"Why didn't you tell us sooner?" demanded Lang.

"I was scared."

"Who? What did they look like?"

She took a shaky breath. "There was a man and a woman. I didn't get a good look at them. But they came and left through his front door."

"Are you sure?" Detective Stewart scribbled notes furiously.

"Yes. I'm next door."

"Did you tell anyone?" asked Lang.

Hadley shook her head.

"When you see something like that, you need to speak up. That's the kind of thing we have to know about."

"Okay. Next time I will."

The detective turned to the officer. "I hope the door-bell cam still has that footage."

"Can I go now?" Hadley rose. "I don't know anything else."

Officer Lang motioned for her to sit. "We have more questions about the two people you saw. And we still need to know where you were that hour on Friday night."

"I'm done. I know you can't hold me without a warrant. I'm also a minor. Pretty sure my parents are supposed to be aware of you interrogating me."

"Questioning you," the detective corrected. "And the school can act as a parent, giving us permission."

"Is that true?"

They both nodded.

Hadley gritted her teeth. They had to be lying. "I have the number of a lawyer my dad gave me. I'm going to call him before I say anything else."

"You can go. If you think of anything else, give us a call."

Lang handed her a card.

The bell rang.

Hadley weaved her way through the crowded halls to the bathroom. Got to a stall just in time to empty her stomach. Ignored the girls calling her bulimic.

The police knew she'd been with Duke right before he died.

And she had no way to make them think she hadn't been with him.

They didn't have proof, but they *knew*. They would probably find some proof in the car. Or on him. Aside from eating, they'd made out, and he'd run his hands all through her hair to fix it before she went backstage.

Her DNA had to be all over his car — and him.

It was only a matter of time until they found it.

Chapter Twenty-One

BRAD FLIPPED through the file waiting in his inbox. His next hit. Again, close to home. Usually, he traveled out of the county — or at least the state — to eliminate his targets. Made it less likely that he'd be recognized.

Now the hits were getting closer to Pine Harbor.

Was Kurt testing him? Brad had made it clear he would never take a job in his hometown.

One more thing to bring up with Kurt, if his boss ever made it back into the office. It was looking more and more doubtful by the day.

"New target?" asked Rose, sitting next to him.

"Yep." He closed the file. "Is Kurt in?"

She scooted closer. "Haven't seen him."

"He's avoiding me."

"You really think he thinks about any of us enough to bother?"

"That's a valid point, but in this case, he really is. He promised me help on *Saturday*. What has he given me? Zilch."

"I wouldn't take it personally." She rested a hand on his leg. "I heard he had a nasty hangover yesterday."

Brad pushed away from her, causing the chair to squeak against the floor.

Was that a smirk?

Rose inched closer. "How's the search going for your dad's killer?"

That gave him pause. He couldn't recall ever mentioning that to her.

She batted her eyelashes. "Didn't you say you were getting close?"

Brad knew he hadn't told her that.

"It must be so frustrating not having answers for so long. It's been, what, thirty years?"

He stood. "I don't have time to look into that while the police are eyeing me for my neighbor's murder."

"You don't have to worry about it. Kurt said he'd take care of that."

"Which means nothing right now."

She gave him a pouty frown. "He won't let you down."

"I'll believe that when I see it." Brad shoved his chair against the table.

A key sounded in the back door.

Kurt entered, his hair unusually disheveled.

"Where have you been?" Brad demanded.

"Hello to you, too."

"The cops are breathing down my throat. Have you seen any of my calls or texts?"

"Of course I have. Stop talking so loudly."

Anger surged through Brad. "They came *here* yesterday. The cops."

Kurt froze.

"If we don't get them off my back, they're going to

start looking at the company. It's bad enough the killer used one of our knives."

"One of *ours*? Which one?"

"The Valderdorf."

Kurt swore. "You'd better get them focused somewhere else — and quickly."

"That's why I've been trying to reach you."

"You should be able to figure this out yourself."

"What?" Brad exclaimed. "You always help out when we get into pickles with the law."

"Regarding *our* jobs." Kurt cracked his knuckles. "This has nothing to do with us."

"Aside from the fact that I'm being framed by someone who used a BlueBlade."

"We don't know someone is framing you."

"I'll let the attorney decide that. So again, I need his number."

"To my office." Kurt unlocked his door.

Brad could hardly believe his luck. His boss wasn't usually so agreeable.

Rose gave him a thumbs-up.

Kurt closed the door. "Have a seat. We need to talk about last Friday."

"That's why I'm here."

"Not your neighbor."

Brad stared at him.

"Your sloppy job."

Of course, it wouldn't be that easy. "I was jumped. I had to fight off attackers on top of taking out the target. If anything, I should get a medal for doing both in one night."

"Excuses."

"Pardon me?"

"You heard fine."

Brad silently counted to ten. "I overcame two people trying to kill me and *still* managed to do my job. Nobody else could have done that, and you know it."

"Why did you have attackers in the first place?"

"You're putting this on me?"

"It's already on you. If this were anyone else, we'd be dealing with a write-up instead of having this discussion."

"Are you kidding me?"

"Do I look like I'm joking?" Kurt's nostrils flared.

Brad chose his words carefully. "I did my best, given my *training*. Nobody else would have managed as well as I did. And I haven't complained."

"Unless multiple calls and texts count."

"You told me on *Saturday* that you'd get me out of this mess. I haven't heard from you since then."

"Because you're impatient." Kurt dramatically sighed.

"The police are breathing down my back, and half my neighbors are eyeing me. It won't be long before BlueBlade is involved."

"And that's my fault?"

"I'm not placing blame, but something needs to be done."

"You should be skilled enough to handle it."

"What I need is your attorney."

Kurt pressed his palms on the desk. "You *need* to remember what's at stake."

"Pardon me?"

"Remember what happened to Felix?"

An icy chill ran through Brad. "You're bringing up the Felix incident?"

"That's what happens when our assassins go off the rails."

"You think I've gone off the rails?"

"Don't ever forget your predecessor."

Brad pulled on his hair.

"Think of your family," Kurt added.

Rage ran through him. It took every ounce of his self-control not to shove everything off his boss's desk and beat the man to a pulp.

A slow smile spread across Kurt's face. "Focus on your new target. Be prepared for anything. And whatever you do, make sure you don't involve the company in your problems — meaning, get the police to stop looking at you ASAP. They start poking around here, and you're really going to have trouble."

"Are you for real?"

"I told you I'm on your side. Do you trust me?"

Not any farther than he could throw the man. "Of course I do."

Kurt cocked a brow. "The Felix incident."

Brad clenched his fists. After a few beats of silence, he left, resisting the urge to slam the door.

"How'd it go?" Rose smiled brightly.

Brad cracked his knuckles, giving himself a moment to collect his thoughts. He'd be fired if he told anyone what he really thought of his boss. "It could've gone better."

"Oh." She frowned. "Anything I can do?"

"No."

"Are you sure?"

He glowered at her.

"No need to be so grumpy. I'm just trying to help."

He grabbed the file for his new target. "I'm working from home for the rest of today."

"I can help you."

"Haven't we been over this?"

"Two minds are better than one, and you trained me. Can't ask for better, right?"

"Fine." Brad was too furious to drive anyway. He sat, slamming his file down.

Rose scooted closer. "How's your family holding up with all the stress? Your wife seemed anxious at the party."

His breath hitched, being reminded of Faye. His wife had made everything worse, not only by lying to the cops but by being the last person Duke saw before his murder.

"She isn't upset with you, is she?" Her lips parted slightly, eyes widening with concern.

"My whole family is upset over the death. It isn't part of their normal lives."

"Understandable. How are you holding up?"

"Fantastic. Can't you tell?"

"Don't let this get to you. You're better than this." She stood behind him and rubbed his shoulders.

"This isn't appropriate." He tried to squirm away.

She tightened her grip and pushed harder. "Don't be such a prude. I'm just trying to help you relax, and liquor isn't allowed during business hours."

He pulled away and leaped to his feet. "It has nothing to do with being a prude. I'm a married man, and I don't feel like having my shoulders massaged. I have a killer to hunt down while, at the same time, plotting to take down my next target."

"Let me help." She turned and met his gaze. "I made progress with some of your neighbors. If I can get together with a few of them, they'll spill facts. It'll be so much easier in a quieter setting."

"Why are you being so helpful?"

Rose inched closer and rubbed his sore muscles again. "You trained me. I wouldn't be half the assassin I am today without you. It's the least I can do."

Guilt stung. If he had been a better protégé, Edmund

Felix would still be alive. "I appreciate that. Sorry for being so rude."

"You're stressed." Her tone dripped like syrup. "I get it."

He started to relax but then stepped away as soon as he realized the situation was easing back into inappropriate territory. "What do you think I should do?"

She pursed her lips and batted her lashes. "You need to stay focused on your assignment. It's going to be too difficult looking into the real killer because of how close you are to everything. Your neighbors like me, so let me handle them. One of them must know something. And if I can get them drinking, they'll be more likely to spill deets."

"You're probably right."

"I definitely am. The last thing you need is extra stress. And it really does seem like he" — she nodded toward Kurt's door — "is putting you off. You need someone on your side. Let that be me."

"Okay. I should get to work." He held up the file. "Looks like this one is going to be especially tricky."

"Figures. I don't know what his problem is lately. But you aren't alone. The last thing you need is to drop the ball on this target."

"I was jumped!"

"Doesn't matter. Kurt will be watching you like a hawk." She pulled out her phone and tapped on the screen before walking away. "Hey, Wes. Glad I caught you. Can we meet later?"

Brad opened the file again and sighed. This hit would make or break his career.

He'd better get it right.

Chapter Twenty-Two

BRAD PUT the last dinner plate in the dishwasher and turned it on. "I'm going to be in my office for a few hours."

Faye closed her laptop. "We need to talk—"

"Again?"

"Let me finish. Hadley needs us."

"She doesn't seem to think so. Her rudeness was off the charts at dinner."

Faye frowned. "You didn't need to send her to her room like a little kid."

"She was acting like one."

"I think she's hurting. We need to figure out what's going on."

"Sounds like the time for a mother-daughter talk. Have fun."

"No. This involves both of us."

Brad's stomach knotted. "Did you catch the part about me needing to work? With all of the distraction about Duke—"

"Did the detective come back to your workplace today?"

"Surprisingly not, but I still can't get anything from Kurt. I get the feeling he doesn't want to help me."

"Well, neither of us are guilty, so it shouldn't be hard to prove."

He tilted his head. "We're lying to the police, Faye. Do you remember that part?"

She glanced around. "Not so loud!"

"You don't want the kids hearing?"

"No."

"Then maybe you shouldn't have lied."

"I was scared!"

He sucked in a deep breath. "I understand. But I need to focus on work for a little while. Give me an hour, then we can talk to Hadley. You can even warm her up before I join you."

"You'd like that." She frowned. "No. I'm really worried about her — and you should be, too. The more I think about the sweatshirt, the more I think she could be involved."

"Not our girl."

"She's practically a woman. Almost eighteen."

"Hadley wasn't involved."

Faye tilted her head. "With what? Duke or the murder?"

It was like a punch to the stomach. "Either. How could you think such a thing?"

"I don't want to, but look at the clues. She's depressed or anxious … and that sweatshirt."

"The one belonging to Maverick?"

"So she says."

"There's no way she's a killer!" He bit back the urge to say he would know if she were. "Or dating a grown man."

"She's pretty enough."

"Hadley's also so busy she doesn't have time. Plays, academic awards, sports — she barely has time to sleep."

Faye put her hand on her hips. "We're talking to her together. You need to man up."

"Excuse me?"

"You heard me."

Brad slammed his hand on the table. "Let's do this, then. Prove to you that I'm right. She's just being a moody teenage girl who's rattled by a murder taking place next door. She's acting perfectly normal for the circumstances."

Faye's expression tightened. Without a word, she marched from the table, then up the stairs.

Brad followed her, eager to get this off his plate. There was still so much he needed to do to prepare for his next target. But every time he dug into it, his mind wandered back to Duke's murder.

If only Duke had been killed when we'd *all been home. Or somewhere with a lot of witnesses.*

"Or if he had never been murdered in the first place," Faye said.

"What?" Brad stared at her. Realization flooded him.

He'd said that last thought out loud.

Crap.

"Don't you agree?" Faye asked.

"Of course, it would've been better if he hadn't been killed. But it's made so much worse by the fact that I wasn't here, and we had to cover for you cutting his hair right before his death."

Her eyes softened. "You have a point. But there's no sense in wishing things were different. We can only deal with the hand we're holding now."

"A hand that sucks."

"But once the killer has been found, everything will go

back to normal. The cops will stop looking at us, and this will all be a distant memory."

Hadley exited her room, eyes widening as she hurried toward the bathroom.

"Wait!" Faye raced toward her. "Your dad and I want to ask you something."

"Right now?" Hadley frowned. "I'm kind of busy. I have a lot of homework, and I need to practice for my next tryout."

"This will only take a minute, sweetheart."

"Can't it wait?"

Brad stood next to Faye. "It really can't, but we'll be quick. I have homework of my own I have to do."

"For what?"

"Work."

"The knife shop gives you homework?" Hadley looked at him in disbelief.

"I have to stay on top of everything for my presentations at conventions and trainings."

"Boring." She opened her bedroom door. "Let's get this over with."

"Yes, let's."

Hadley plopped on her bed. "This isn't about the sweatshirt, is it? I can show you pictures of Maverick if that'll make you feel better."

"That isn't what this is about." Faye sat and put her arm around Hadley. "Although, it's part of it."

"Am I in trouble?"

"No. We just have some questions. We're worried about you."

Hadley threw her father a pleading look.

"Give us reason *not* to worry," Mom said.

"I'm fine. Just busy."

Faye leaned closer and took Hadley's hand. "Are kids bugging you at school about the investigation?"

Hadley shook her head. "Nobody's saying anything to me."

"Nobody?"

She chewed on her lower lip. "Well, that detective asked me some questions at school today."

Brad could hardly believe his ears. "She what?"

"I was called into the office, and they asked me some questions."

"What did she say?" Brad chewed on his bottom lip. "And why weren't we informed?"

"She said the school could allow it in your place."

"That can't be right." He shook his head.

Hadley shrugged. "That's what she said."

"What did she ask you?"

"Not much. I told her I had a lawyer's number, and that was the end of that."

"She backed off once you said that?"

"Basically. Can I finish my homework now?"

"She didn't ask anything that made you uncomfortable?" Brad asked. "Any accusations?"

"Nope. Just curious, I guess. Can I go?"

"We still need to know about Duke. How well did you know him?"

"How well does anyone know another person?"

"Hadley," Faye warned.

She sighed dramatically. "We talked sometimes. He gave me tips on my singing."

"He what?" Brad exclaimed.

Faye narrowed her eyes at him.

Hadley played with her hair. "Duke had helped his sister with voice lessons or something. When he heard me practicing in the backyard, he offered some tips."

"And you never told us?" Brad asked.

"It wasn't a big deal, but I knew you'd make it one. Like you are now."

"It's okay, honey," Faye said quickly.

Brad glared at her, not that she was looking his way. She'd dragged him into this conversation, and now she was making him out to be the bad guy for asking questions. He shoved his fists into his pockets. "Looks like we're done here."

Faye's eyes widened.

"Unless you have anything else you want to ask."

She shifted her weight on the bed before turning to their daughter. "Do you mind if we have a look at the sweatshirt?"

"What sweatshirt?" Hadley looked around.

Brad held back an eye roll. For a top performer at her school, she was a terrible actress right now. "The one we were talking about this morning."

"Oh. You mean Maverick's."

"Right."

"Haven't you guys already seen it? I mean, you snooped in here and gave me the third degree this morning."

Faye's mouth dropped open. "I was not snooping. It was out in the open. I came in here to find you, and it was on your chair. Snooping would be if you'd hidden it and I found it."

Hadley frowned.

"Where did you meet Maverick?"

"I told you. School. Want to see a picture of us together?"

Brad shook his head. "Your mother asked to see the sweatshirt."

"Fine." She scrambled over to her closet and dug

through it.

Faye leaned forward, practically on the verge of falling off the bed.

Brad just waited. It wasn't like they were going to learn anything from the shirt. Hadley had probably already washed off the cologne before he or Faye got home. Teenagers never discussed their love lives with their parents. It was just one of those things. He'd never mentioned Faye to his mom and stepdad until things got serious until she'd wanted to meet his family.

Hadley pulled out the sweatshirt. "See? Same as this morning. No big deal."

A folded piece of paper fell from the pocket.

Faye scrambled to her feet. "What's that?"

"Nothing." Hadley's face paled.

Brad inched closer. "Doesn't look like nothing to me."

She snatched it from the floor and put it behind her back. "Well, it is."

"Let us see that."

"No."

"Hadley, we're all in this together. We have to prove our innocence *as a family*."

"It's nothing." She backed up so that she was inside the closet.

"If it's no big deal, hand it over."

"Leave me alone!"

Brad reached for her. "Hand it over. We aren't going to ground you if that's what you're worried about. The only thing we're concerned about is the truth — especially with the cops snooping around, asking us all questions."

Hadley shook her head.

Faye reached for her. "We aren't going anywhere, honey. Let us see the paper, so we can figure this out together."

Tears shone in Hadley's eyes. "Duke and I were in love! Are you happy now?"

The room simultaneously spun and shrunk around him.

Faye had been right.

Their baby girl had been dating that predator. "What did he do to you?"

"Nothing! He never hurt me. Not once."

"*Hurt* you?" Brad clenched his fists, struggled to breathe. "He hurt you?"

"I just said he didn't." The tears were coming fast now.

His anger melted, and his heart broke for his daughter. What had that monster put her through? He pulled Hadley to his chest and clung to her. "What made you jump to him hurting you?"

"*Not hurting me.*" Her voice was smooshed.

He relaxed his grip. "Why was that the word you jumped to?"

"Because that's what you were insinuating! Duke was always a perfect gentleman. He was so much nicer than any of the boys my age. They're all a bunch of Neanderthals. If you're worried about somebody bothering me, those are the idiots who deserve your concern."

"What did the boys at school do to you?" he demanded.

"What don't they do?" She threw her father an exasperated look. "They pretend to hug us from behind to cop a feel. That sort of thing. And they know how to do it so the teachers won't notice."

Faye gasped. "Even with all the no-touching rules they have?"

Hadley rolled her eyes. "They always think up ways to get around it. Duke wasn't like that. Ever." Fat tears spattered down her cheeks. "You couldn't have asked for someone to treat me better than he did."

"He never touched you?" Brad demanded.

She wiped her eyes and sniffled. "Don't ask what you don't want to know."

Like an arrow to his heart. He stumbled backward, the world spinning out of control.

It was a good thing Duke was already dead. Otherwise, Brad would march next door and kill the predator himself. Any judge in their right mind would side with him.

"Why didn't you tell us?" Faye asked.

Hadley leaned against the wall and slid to a sitting position, clinging to the sweatshirt. "Because I knew you'd freak out like you are now."

Faye knelt in front of her. "We just want to take care of you."

"Oh yeah? Dad looks like he's going to pass out from anger."

"I think he's taking in the news." She squeezed their daughter's knee. "Are you okay?"

Hadley buried her face in the sweatshirt and shook her head no. "My boyfriend is dead."

In love. Boyfriend. It was like she was trying to end him with her words.

"We're getting you into counseling," Faye said. "There's no way you can deal with this on your own."

Her answer for everything.

But this time, Brad wasn't about to object. His daughter needed an anti-brainwashing program after having been deceived by a predator.

"Great," Hadley mumbled. "Can you guys leave me alone now?"

"After you answer one more question."

She looked up, makeup smeared across her face. "Then you'll go?"

Faye nodded. "You weren't involved with his death, were you?"

"Mom! No, of course not. Never. We were going to get engaged after my graduation."

Brad struggled to breathe.

Faye's eyes widened. "You had marriage plans?"

"Engagement."

"That's crazy," Brad said. "You're too young to be thinking about any of that."

"Really?" Hadley narrowed her eyes. "You and Mom got married when she was twenty."

Faye covered her mouth.

Brad struggled to take a deep breath, to think of something to say. Not that it mattered. Duke was dead. The pervert couldn't marry his baby.

It was all in the past.

Hadley leaped to her feet. "I answered your question, now go!"

Faye reached for their daughter. "But I—"

She darted away. "No. I have to be alone now. I'll do counseling or whatever, but I can't deal with this — with you two — right now."

Brad put his arm around Faye, his pulse racing in his ear. "Let's give her space." He glanced back at Hadley. "This is far from over."

Chapter Twenty-Three

FAYE CLOSED THE BEDROOM DOOR, memories of their early years of marriage strobing through her mind. Brad throwing things across the room. Punching a hole in a wall, a door, a dresser. Flying off the handle for no reason. Screaming at her because he'd imagined a reaction she hadn't given him.

All baggage from his past, all aimed at her. It damaged her deeply.

It had taken years of therapy to heal, to get past it all. And even now, Brad still had a temper. He just knew how to control it these days.

Not that it could change the past. The wasted years. Her early twenties could have been spent having fun and finding herself. Instead, she'd been avoiding flying objects and learning how to avoid his fury — by trial and error, usually discovering some deep-rooted trigger by accident. His words and tone like a slap to the face.

If she hadn't gotten pregnant with Hadley, her twenties would've been a total waste. Faye had been dedicated to Brad, to their marriage. She felt bad for him, knowing all

he'd endured. She'd been there with him through the aftermath of his dad's murder.

It had forged a bond between them — Faye, the
soother, Brad, the wounded soul. As soon as they married,
all his vitriol was aimed at her, as though she had been the
enemy. Not his father's murderer. Not his mother, who
never thought counseling would help him.

Faye had been the one to prove her mother-in-law
wrong. Their therapist had done wonders. Granted, it took
a while. At first, Brad wouldn't go. Then he resisted help
even after he did. Laughed at the suggestions. But when
Faye packed her suitcase, Brad finally realized the severity
of his problem.

Begged, pleaded, promised change. Finally, he stepped
up and took the doctor's advice seriously. Learned to put
the past behind him — where it belonged — and, as a
result, had less anger day to day. Stopped taking everything
out on her.

But still, nothing could ever bring back the wasted
years.

She would never admit it out loud, but given the
chance to go back in time, she would do things differently.
How, she wasn't sure. Faye loved their children with all her
heart and could never imagine life without them. It would
be incomplete. And she couldn't have Hadley or Luna or
Zeke without Brad.

Faye imagined demanding change earlier. Packing bags
years before she did. Getting professional help for herself
despite his early insistence that such a thing was only for
the weak. A crutch for losers.

It killed her that she'd tolerated so much. Wasted the
best years of her life, living in fear, always walking on
eggshells, not knowing when he would blow up next.

And now Hadley wanted to marry young. To risk the

same heartache when she had her entire life in front of her. She could spend her twenties traveling the world, getting to know herself, exploring what life had to offer.

But instead—

"Faye?" Brad waved his hand in front of her.

"Stop." She glared at him, regret transforming into irritation.

"We have to talk about this."

"I know." Faye stumbled to the bed and collapsed onto it, barely feeling the blankets supporting her.

"Our daughter was sneaking around with that predator next door!"

"Nothing we can do about that now." Relief washed through her. Hadley had been spared the heartache Faye had endured for so long. Sure, she'd have her own demons to fight. Losing a boyfriend to murder would haunt her for years — not unlike Brad and his father. But she would get professional help. She wouldn't abuse anyone with her own wounds. She wouldn't have the regrets that her mother had been forced to live with.

She'd been spared. Given a new chance at life.

"You don't look nearly as worried as I do," Brad accused.

Faye blinked a few times. Stared at her red-faced husband.

"Well?"

"I'm processing the news. Give me a minute."

He turned away. "At least you aren't saying *I told you so*."

"I'm not a toddler."

Brad tugged on his hair. "What are we going to do?"

"I'm going to make counseling appointments for all of us first thing in the morning."

"Great, but I mean, what are *we* going to do?"

"About what?"

He looked at her like she was crazy. "Hadley!"

"We need to be there for her. Can you imagine what she's going through right now? The love of her life was murdered. She's only seventeen. I don't know how she's managing."

"She was also abused. Groomed by a child predator."

"We don't know that it was like that. They may have just fallen in love."

"He was twenty-five, and she's only seventeen!"

"That's the legal age in some states."

He glowered at her. "Not here."

"There was a time you were an adult, and I was a minor."

"We only had a two-year age gap, and we met in high school. It's totally different. I never took advantage of you."

"It isn't that different."

"Are you serious?"

"Young love is blind."

His nostrils flared. "What she's experiencing is abuse, not love."

"And she'll be in counseling. Daily, if necessary. But she'll be fine."

He paced, stopping just in front of her. "Why don't you seem concerned about this?"

Her heart skipped a beat. The last thing she wanted was to voice her marital regrets. "Of course I am! Who insisted we talk to her about the sweatshirt?"

"You were a lot more concerned before she admitted to sleeping with the *man* next door."

Faye took a deep breath. "It's over, Brad. He's dead. It's impossible for her to go back to him. We need to be concerned with getting her grief counseling."

"*Grief* counseling? Try abuse recovery. This is going to mess her up for life."

"Therapy helped you! You're a completely different man from the person you were when we first married."

"Stop trying to compare her with us. Not even on the same playing field."

She stared him down.

His lips pursed. "Is there something you want to say to me?"

"No."

"You sure?"

"That's what I just said."

Brad threw his hands up in the air. "I can't believe this."

"What?"

"I see what you're doing!"

"What?" she repeated.

The silence felt like a lead weight pressing on her.

"You're glad she doesn't have to stay with the same man she chose young. Like you did."

Faye's stomach dropped. "I didn't say that."

"You didn't *have* to!" Spittle flew from his mouth.

"Brad, you know I love you. The life we've built together. I wouldn't exchange anything we have."

"Anything we have *now*, right?"

She swallowed.

"I knew it."

Bile rose in her mouth.

"Can't deny it, can you?"

"I love you. Everything we have together."

"But you settled."

"It's not like that—"

"I need to get some air." He stormed out of the room, slamming the door behind him.

Chapter Twenty-Four

BRAD FLUNG himself on the barstool and ordered a beer without looking at the bartender. His mind raced, unable to believe his wife of twenty-three years still regretted marrying him.

Hadn't they gotten past that years ago?

Apparently not. She hadn't even tried to convince him that he was wrong.

All she was concerned about was that Hadley wouldn't make the same mistake she'd made. Marrying him.

Twenty-three years together. And for what?

He gulped down the drink as soon as it appeared in front of him. Ordered another. He would drain the bar if he could.

How could the regret be her takeaway from this situation? Their daughter had been groomed and abused by a man who pretended to be a stand-up guy.

What would the neighbors say if they knew what Duke was really like?

They'd say Brad killed him. That he had more motive than anyone ever imagined.

And they wouldn't be wrong. Except that he'd had no clue and never had the opportunity to kill his daughter's abuser.

Brad took the next drink and sipped it. Needed to think. Couldn't do that if he got drunk.

Then he'd do something to really make Faye regret marrying him.

Maybe that wasn't such a bad thing. She was already regretting him. Why not go all the way?

He chugged the rest of his beer and waved at the bartender for another.

Relaxation massaged his muscles.

That sent red hot irritation through him. Good. He didn't want to be relaxed. Needed to stay angry and clear-headed.

Which meant this new drink was his last.

"Are you okay?" asked a feminine voice next to him.

He turned to see who was flirting with him.

Detective Stewart. Glowering, not flirting.

"I'm fine." He turned back to his drink.

"You're drinking like a fish."

He held up the glass. "It's only my third one. Is that illegal?"

She shook her head. "But it's a lot for five minutes."

"Who asked you?"

"Do you need a ride home?"

He snorted. "You'd like that, huh? I'm not answering any of your questions. And speaking of that — leave my kids alone. You don't get to talk to them without my permission. My daughter wasn't joking about calling an attorney."

The detective nodded.

"What are you doing here, anyway? Following me?"

"Here on another case."

"Don't let me interrupt you."

She smirked. "You're not."

He turned from her and sipped his drink, not caring what she thought. Probably should a little since his goal was getting her off his back, but he didn't.

"Tell me more about the Valderdorf knife."

"It's rare." He took another sip, staring at the rows of alcohol on the shelves behind the bar.

"How rare?"

"Mostly owned by collectors." He twisted his glass in a circle. "And people from the company, but you could call most of us collectors."

"What's so special about it?"

"The blade is cobalt blue, like all of our blades." It was so easy to slip into salesman mode. He could discuss the knives in a drunken stupor, and he had only a buzz at the moment. "But the Valderdorf has a unique curve to the blade. Most people choose to display theirs, but plenty use them as well. The knife works as well on meat as on heated butter."

"Really?"

He turned to the detective. "I'm surprised you don't know this. It's hardly classified information. You can find that and more on our website."

She pulled out her tablet and made a note. Hopefully, that meant she'd be leaving him alone. "Do you have a Valderdorf?"

He sighed. "Yes."

"And do you display yours?"

"A few in my private collection. Mostly, we use our BlueBlades."

"So, what exactly do you display? I don't recall seeing any in your home."

"Do you want a complete list? I don't know all of them

offhand."

She studied him with an unreadable expression.

Or maybe it would be readable if he hadn't just emptied three glasses of beer. If he'd known she was going to show up, he'd have at least slowed down. "Is that everything?"

"Did Duke have a Valderdorf?"

"How would I know?"

The detective cleared her throat. "Did you sell him one?"

"That would be a no."

"I thought you two were friendly."

"We had friendly competitions," Brad clarified. "I never once said we were friends. Just neighbors. You know how people are these days. Barely wave at the people next door, much less know the names of everyone on their street. Welcome to the twenty-first century."

"Yet you had your neighborhood over for a party this weekend?"

He gritted his teeth. "It was a Super Bowl party. Neighborhood tradition. Duke had been hosting them since he moved in. Faye and I thought we'd try to boost the community morale by making sure it went on in his honor."

"In Duke's honor?" She made more notes.

Brad wanted to get up and leave, but she'd only follow him. "That's what I said."

"Anything else you can tell me about the knife?"

"Like I said, it's on the website. Do you need the URL?"

"No thanks."

"So, you'll be going now?"

"I find it interesting that a rare knife from your company was used."

He shrugged. "A lot of people in my neighborhood buy BlueBlades."

"Really?"

"I do talk about them when people ask about my work." He finished his drink.

"How often does that happen?"

Brad shrugged. "It tends to come up in conversations when people move in. But I'm not pushy about it like Duke always was with his supplements."

"He was pushy?"

"Maybe that's too strong a word." He drew in a deep breath. "He was a top MLM marketer, so he knew how to bring his products into a conversation. I'm sure it was just natural for him to mention it with neighbors."

"And you don't know if he owned one of your knives?"

"Like I said, I wouldn't know."

She pushed her stool back.

Finally.

"If you think of anything else, give me a call." She handed him another card.

"I already have one. Two, actually."

"Then this will make it a collection." She smiled before walking away.

Brad shook his head and turned back to his empty glass.

"Refill?" asked the bartender.

"Not yet." Everything was already spinning around him, and not from the alcohol. He rubbed his temples, wishing he'd thought to take some ibuprofen earlier.

"Brad?"

He spun around. "Rose, what are you doing here?"

"Remember? I said I was coming here to talk to your neighbor."

"You did?"

"At work."

"It's been a seriously long evening."

She frowned, her lower lip protruding to look more like a pout. "I'm sorry. Want to talk about it?"

He shrugged and turned back to his empty glass.

"Hungry?" Rose took the detective's stool.

Brad mumbled something not even he understood.

"That settles it. We're eating. My treat."

He shook his head.

"Come on." When he didn't budge, she grabbed his hand and pulled him from the stool. Her fingers laced through his, and though he tried to pull away, her grip was like that of a professional bodybuilder.

The bartender said something about Brad's tab.

"Add it to mine." Rose smiled widely, and she pointed behind her. "We'll be sitting over there."

Brad tried to pull his hand away from hers, annoyed at her impossible strength. Or had the beers weakened his resolve? It wasn't like he'd downed that many.

She dragged him to a table near the back with a pale pink coat draped over one of the chairs. "This is where I sat with a couple of your neighbors. Sit."

He stared at the table with two nearly empty plates of food.

"You poor thing." Rose finally removed her intertwined fingers from his, then she wrapped her arms around him, squishing herself against him. "I saw that detective talking to you. She still thinks you're guilty?"

Brad struggled free from her grasp. "Pretty much."

Her eyes filled with pity as she kissed his cheek. "You're getting it from all sides. Sit down and tell me all about it."

"Only for a minute." Brad sat across from her, eager to get somewhere he could wallow in his pity alone. If only he could think straight enough to figure out where.

Chapter Twenty-Five

Faye splashed cold water on her face and stared in the mirror. It still looked like she'd been crying, but at least her makeup wasn't smeared across her face anymore. She needed to get Luna ready for bed and didn't want her young daughter to know she was upset. There was enough going on without distressing her more. She was the only one who didn't really understand what was happening.

After checking on the older two — both holed up in their rooms — Faye made her way downstairs, where Luna was still watching cartoons in the living room.

Ding-dong!

Faye groaned.

"Who's here, Mommy?"

"I'm not sure. Keep watching your show."

"Really?" Her eyes went bright. "I don't have to get ready for bed?"

"After I see who's here." Faye kissed her on the top of the head and hurried down the hall, only stopping to check her reflection. She had bags under her eyes, and her hair was limp, but she wasn't trying to win a beauty contest.

Allison stood outside.

Faye's stomach knotted. Her friend would know something was wrong as soon as she opened the door. She'd have to come up with a lie. Hopefully, a better one than she'd concocted for the police over the weekend.

She flung open the door, but Allison didn't even look at Faye before rushing in.

"Come in." She closed the door.

"Where's Brad?" Allison looked around.

"He's out."

"At a bar?" She finally turned to Faye. "Are you okay?"

"Yeah, fine. Why would you think he's at a bar?"

Allison stepped closer. "Wes just called me from the one by the lake."

"And he saw Brad there?"

"You don't look surprised."

Faye waved her friend toward the kitchen and poured two glasses of sparkling water. She would've preferred wine, but Allison was expecting. "We've been under stress. Brad wanted some time alone."

"Alone, huh?" Allison lifted a brow and sipped her drink.

"That's what he said. Did he run into someone there?"

She held Faye's gaze for a moment. "Rose."

Faye's heart plummeted. "What?"

Allison frowned. "I hate to be the one to tell you, but it's true."

The floor disappeared beneath her. She leaned on the island for support. Tried to think of something to say. Wes had to be wrong. Or he was covering for himself. He'd definitely been flirting with Rose the other night. They'd probably met at the bar, and Brad had only stopped to say hi to his co-worker.

Yeah, that had to be it. Brad was pissed when he'd left,

but not *that* pissed. Their problems weren't that bad. They'd survived so much worse.

"You aren't worried?"

"No. I trust Brad."

Allison chewed on her lower lip and looked conflicted.

"What?"

"I don't know if I should tell you. I mean, I probably should, but I hate to be the bearer of bad news."

"Spill it."

Allison drew a deep breath. "They were holding hands."

"What?" The room took on a crimson hue.

"I'm sorry, sweetie." Allison outstretched her arms and headed around the island.

"You're wrong."

"I wish I was."

"No! You are."

"Oh, Faye. I wish I was, but I have proof. Wes got a picture."

She gasped for air, clung to the counter.

Allison showed her a picture of Brad and Rose strolling through a bar, hand in hand.

It was true.

"It gets worse."

Faye closed her eyes. She didn't want to know. But she needed the truth. "What?"

"Wes says she kissed him."

"Rose *kissed* my husband? On the lips?"

"On the cheek."

A fire burned in her. She stood tall, her eyes narrowed. "Show me the picture."

"He didn't get that on camera."

Faye stumbled back. "I'm going to call him. You need to leave."

"You need moral support." Allison hesitated.

"Is there anything else?"

"Unfortunately."

"Tell me, then leave."

Allison opened her mouth, didn't say anything.

"Spill it!"

"She slipped something into his pocket." Allison backed away.

"I need you to go."

"Don't call him!"

"Why the hell not?"

Allison took a few steps closer. "Go down there. Confront him in person. Confront them both. Let it be known you're a force to reckoned with."

Faye sucked in a few ragged breaths. "You're right."

"Of course I am. Now what you need is—"

"I can handle this." She darted past Allison and into the living room. "Luna, honey, I have to run out somewhere real quick. I need you to get yourself ready for bed after this show is over."

Luna's eyes widened.

"If you need something, ask Hadley or Zeke for help. I won't be gone long."

"Mommy?" Fear shone in her eyes.

"Everything is going to be okay." Faye squeezed her, hoping that was the truth. Then she hurried upstairs to tell the older kids she was leaving.

On the way to the bar, her stomach did somersaults, and she had to turn on the AC to cool her body. The image of Rose and Brad holding hands was burned into her mind. Constantly flashing into her thoughts.

How could things have spiraled so quickly? Everything had been fine before the murder. Okay, maybe not *every-*

thing, but good enough. Better than most marriages of their vintage.

She raced into the building. Before opening the door, she paused. She didn't even know what she would say to them.

What would she do if Brad admitted to betraying her? Or worse, if he wanted to end things? To destroy their family?

Hot, angry tears threatened, but she blinked them all back. She wouldn't let either of them see her crying.

Faye was anything but weak. She was a woman scorned.

Nothing would take her down. No one.

She took a few deep breaths and determined to stay classy. If anyone was going to fly off the handle, it wasn't going to be her.

Inside, she squinted in the bright lights. Nearly had to cover her ears to dampen the loud music, the pool balls crashing into each other, and the rowdy conversations all around.

Brad wasn't anywhere in sight. Maybe it had all been a mistake. Even the picture Allison showed her could've been faked.

Her husband had been right about one thing — Allison clearly didn't like him. What if this was all a joke to ruin their marriage? She hardly ever came around before Duke's murder.

Faye was ready to turn around and leave when she saw them. Brad and his busty co-worker sitting together at a booth near the back, tucked away from everything else.

The perfect place for a couple to sit if they didn't want to be noticed.

But they'd been noticed. First by Wes, and now by her.

Rage tore through her with enough force that Faye

could pull that woman out of the seat and hurl her across the room.

She stormed over, her mind racing.

Her husband and that home-wrecker were too deep in conversation to even notice her approach.

They both looked at her as she leaned on the table.

Brad's eyes widened, and his face paled. "Faye."

"Yes, it's me. Surprise, surprise."

He scrambled out of the booth. "This isn't what it looks like."

"No?" Her voice rose several octaves. "You aren't sitting here with Rose, enjoying a nice dinner after we had a serious argument?"

Rose covered her mouth.

"Oh, give it up." Faye shot her daggers with her eyes before turning back to her husband. "And sushi? Really? Is the real reason you never would eat that with me because it's your thing with *her*?"

"It's not mine!"

"Sure it isn't. The plate is just sitting in front of you for decoration."

Brad put his hand on her arm, but she jerked away from him. He pleaded with his eyes. "I'm telling the truth. She was here with someone else and invited me over to talk."

Faye snorted. "To *talk*. I'm sure."

He started to say something, but that was when she noticed the lipstick just above his beard. Same color as the hooker-red on Rose's lips.

She slapped him across the face.

Brad covered the spot. "Faye!"

"Whose lipstick is on your face? Funny how it matches hers!" Faye glared at Rose, barely holding herself back from throttling the woman.

He only shook his head.

"Sushi, lipstick. Don't worry — you don't *have* to say anything. It's all crystal clear. Let me check one more thing."

"Faye, you don't understand."

"Sure I don't. How long have I misunderstood our vows?"

"That isn't fair!"

"No?" She reached for his jacket and dug into his pockets. The first one only had his cell phone and keys. The second one had a lighter, with a rose etched into both sides. "What's this?"

"It isn't mine. I've never seen it before!" He turned to Rose.

She shrugged.

Brad grabbed it and threw it across the floor. "See? It means nothing to me."

Faye glowered at Rose. "I hope you're happy."

"I'm so sorry about the confusion." Rose stood, frowning. "It's like Brad said, I was here talking to Tristan about where *he* was the night of the murder — he has a really shaky alibi, by the way — when I saw Brad. Neither of us knew the other was here. He was upset about the detective questioning him, so I invited him here to talk about Tristan. That's all. Brad didn't eat any sushi or anything."

Faye held back the urge to punch her. Hitting her husband was one thing, but it would be assault if she pummeled this woman like she wanted to. "What about the lipstick?"

"It's nothing. Growing up in Spain, everyone kisses everyone on the cheek. I didn't think anything of it. I apologize that it upset you."

"And the picture of you two holding hands?"

Brad's mouth dropped open.

"Wes was looking out for me. Sent Allison a picture."

Brad glanced around, his gaze stopping at their neighbor.

Wes gave a friendly wave.

Brad returned the gesture by flipping him the bird.

Their neighbor's mouth curved up.

Faye turned back to Rose. "You can leave. You've caused enough trouble."

"I'm sorry. I really didn't mean anything by it. I was just trying to help."

"You need a lesson in the meaning of the word *help*." She turned back to her husband. "You still haven't explained your hand-holding escapade."

"She was just leading me over to the table. It was nothing."

"Really?" Faye countered. "So, you wouldn't mind if I went over to Wes there and held his hand? Because it would be nothing. Maybe I could kiss his cheek and slip something into his pocket, too. All nothing, right? Wouldn't bother you at all?"

Brad glanced back and forth between her and Rose.

"Don't look at her!" Faye dug her heels into the floor.

"I'm going to leave." Rose gathered her coat and purse. "Sorry for everything. See you tomorrow, Brad."

Faye's blood was lava bubbling over the lip of a boiling volcano.

Brad turned to her. "Let's discuss this at home."

"You'll talk with Rose publicly, but not me? Classy, Brad."

His brows furrowed. "Everything I said was the truth. Are you really surprised that Wes and Allison are behind this?"

"Don't bring them into this. *You're* the one at a bar with Rose."

"I know this looks terrible, but I'm telling you the truth. I'd never do anything to risk losing what we have together. I swear it."

She glared at him. "I'll talk to you privately, but not at home. Not where the kids could overhear."

"My car?" he offered.

Faye could feel the patrons staring. "Fine."

He took his coat from her, and they headed outside for what might be their last conversation outside of a courtroom.

Chapter Twenty-Six

HADLEY CLOSED Luna's bedroom door and brushed some hair from her eyes. How dare her parents treat her like that, then have the gall to make her get Luna ready for bed.

It was barbaric. Selfish. They acted like they were so perfect, but they weren't.

The way they whispered together like they were hiding something.

Maybe they were.

She went to the front and looked outside. Both cars were still gone.

This was her chance to do some snooping of her own. They'd gone through her things, now it was time for her to do the same. Figure out what they were trying to hide.

Hadley almost stopped in Zeke's room to find out if he wanted to help, but she didn't feel like trying to get his attention while he was playing his video game. That was all he cared about, so why interrupt him?

She tiptoed past Luna's room. If she heard a floor-board creak, she'd cry out for another glass of water or a story or something. It took so long to get that girl into bed.

It made her never want to have children. She definitely didn't want to raise kids like her parents raised her. Both Zeke and Luna had gotten the better end of everything. Her brother barely remembered the days when all her parents did was fight, when Dad used to throw things and scream. When Mom would scream right back.

That was no environment for a child, for anyone. But they'd subjected her to that when she was Luna's age and even younger.

Would she and Duke have had kids? It was a thought that'd passed through her mind so many times when they dreamed out loud about their future together, but she didn't want to scare him off. He liked talking about getting engaged when she was old enough, but for some reason, it felt like bringing up kids could freak him out.

She never knew what was going to set a guy off. Even though she'd never seen Duke lose his cool, she didn't want to risk it.

She would never make the same mistakes as Mom.

Hadley pushed her parents' bedroom door.

Creak!

Her breath hitched. She waited for Luna to call out.

But she didn't.

Heart hammering, Hadley crept into the room. Reached for the light switch but stopped. Didn't want the light on now. Not when someone could see it. A neighbor could mention it to them later — unlikely but possible. More likely, her brother or sister might see it and say something.

Then what? Hadley just wanted to stay off her parents' radar, if possible.

Unless she had something she could confront *them* with.

And they were in no position to complain since they had made such a big deal about Duke's sweatshirt. Not to mention the love letter that had fallen out of it.

Her face burned at the thought. At least she'd managed to keep them from reading it or asking about the others. She would never be able to look at them again if they knew the things she'd written to him.

If they were cool like some of her friends' parents, they'd get it. They wouldn't even care. But her parents had probably never even been in love. Had no idea the amazing euphoria of having someone who thought the world revolved around you.

Hadley pushed those thoughts aside and shined her phone's flashlight around. Nothing looked out of place. The room was tidy — just the way Mom liked things. She was not a fan of clutter or mess. Not like when Hadley was little. But as much as Dad had yelled all the time, Mom had been too busy placating Dad's temper to care about that stuff.

She shoved the thoughts aside again, hating when those memories pushed their way to the surface. Those years were the worst. Having a temper like that should be a misdemeanor or something. Did the police not think screaming at people was damaging?

There was a time she'd wished someone would just hit her. Then she would have proof of her abuse. She knew that was what it felt like. But she'd been too young to know for sure, to trust her own feelings. Even the stupid therapist never gave it that label. But she'd found it online — verbal abuse, mental abuse, emotional abuse. There were all kinds of abuses that left no visible marks but had scarred her soul nonetheless.

She picked up a book from Dad's shelf and threw it across the room. That felt better. Not that it could change anything. Definitely not her ruined childhood. Years she would never get back. All she could hope for was to make a life for herself. A life so wonderful she could forget her formative years.

So far, she was doing well. Starring in school plays, debate team, singing, and on the varsity team for every sport she played. Hadley accomplished whatever she put her mind to—

Stop!

She didn't want to think about any of this. The past was done. The only thing she wanted to think about was figuring out what really happened with Duke. Not that looking through her parents' things was likely to give her answers to who killed him. They'd been clueless about her relationship. Neither of them would've been behind the murder.

But now that they knew, they'd be watching her like a hawk.

Except they'd left the house with her in charge.

Even knowing she was capable of going behind their backs, they still trusted her.

They made no sense whatsoever.

Hadley wasn't about to complain. But she did need to get out of her own head and see what she could find, even if this room was a bust.

She pulled open the bottom chest of drawers. Mom's pants. Nothing. Not even in the pockets. Next one over was Dad's pants. Again, nothing. The entire drawer was perfectly useless.

Same for their nightstands.

The closet.

Under the bed.

Her parents were seriously the most boring people for at least three counties.

Dad's office. He not only kept that locked but with a code.

She'd seen him punch the numbers a few days ago.

Probably couldn't replicate it. But there was only one way to find out.

Her mouth dried as she crept down the hall. She could get caught. If Dad was hiding something in there, he probably had a camera and might get alerted the moment she tried to get in.

Good.

He shouldn't hide things. He'd been the one to teach them all about the value of honesty.

She glanced into Zeke's room as she passed by. Still on his computer. Luna's room. Her sister was sleeping, finally. And their parents' cars were still gone.

This was her chance. If Dad was hiding anything, it would be behind this door.

Her hand shook as she reached for the little code box. The buttons were so small. She thought back to Dad pressing them. Four, six, zero, eight.

Or had it been five?

There was only one option. Try it.

She steadied her hand, listened.

All was quiet.

Her heart was a jackhammer. She took quick breaths. Focused.

If anyone could do this, it was her.

She pressed the five.

Nothing happened.

Was that good? She couldn't remember what the buttons did when Dad set the lock the other morning.

She pressed the six.

The Enter button.

Again, nothing.

Zero. Eight.

The buttons all lit up. Buzzed harshly for a moment.

Nothing else. No clicking of a lock releasing.

Maybe she'd done something wrong. The first number probably *was* a four.

And Dad might've been alerted already.

She needed to hurry.

Four. Six. Zero. Eight.

Enter.

The buttons all flashed. No harsh buzzing.

Click.

Her heart leaped into her throat.

Had it worked?

She turned the knob.

The door opened.

She was in Dad's office.

He had to know now.

But she was here. He wasn't.

Hadley slipped inside, leaving the door cracked. Nearly turned on the light before she caught herself. Didn't want to deal with him finding out from Luna or a neighbor that the light had been on if he didn't have alerts set up on his phone.

Maybe he didn't. It was possible.

Not likely, but possible.

She whipped out her phone. No messages or calls from Dad.

Maybe he didn't know.

Or he was furiously driving home, ready to rip her a new one.

Hadley had the advantage of time. She shone her light all around. A desk, paintings, and knives displayed on the wall, a shelf displaying some of those stupid blue knives he loved so much. A few bags on the floor.

It all looked innocent enough.

Looks could be deceiving.

And so could he.

She hurried over to the desk. Pulled on a drawer.

Locked.

They all were.

Dad was definitely hiding something. Locks behind a locked door.

She tried them all again. Glanced outside. Couldn't really see the driveway from this window. Cracked open the door and listened.

Just her brother hollering at another gamer geek.

Hadley went to the closet. He'd probably rigged the doors to lock.

The door slid open. She directed light into the closet.

Stumbled back. Covered her mouth.

There was a collection of swords and other weapons she couldn't name. Some of them looked medieval. They all looked deadly. Some were rusted.

Like they'd been used a lot.

Why did her dad have all of these? Locked away, no less?

Those weren't hunting knives. They also weren't the knives he showed for work. None of them had that *cobalt* blue he always bragged about other companies trying to copy but never being able to match.

What the hell was he hiding?

Hadley snapped a few pictures for proof. She might doubt herself the next day. Or she might need to confront Dad.

She glanced back out the window, still not seeing her parents' cars. Not that she'd know if they had pulled into the driveway.

Shaking, she studied the weapons up close. All shiny aside from the rare rust spots.

Slam!

She straightened her back.

Front door?

Stumbled back.

A strap wrapped around her ankle.

Tripped over a bag. It rattled like it was full of swords.

Thud!

Pain shot through her tailbone. She cried out.

Covered her mouth.

Scrambled to her feet. Hurried out of the room.

Barely remembered to punch in the code.

Chapter Twenty-Seven

"PUT YOUR PHONE AWAY!"

Hadley shoved the device into her pocket, put her hand back on her stomach, and watched her teammates running back and forth for practice. She wasn't pretending to be sick, but that wasn't the story she'd given the coach. He squirmed whenever one of the girls mentioned it being that time of the month. That was all she'd needed to say for him to let her sit the afternoon's practice out.

The more she thought about her father's office, the worse she felt. Her stomach was churning so much acid she was sure it would burn a hole through her flesh.

Not only did she have to deal with her boyfriend's murder, it now looked like her dad might be involved. What if he'd found out about her relationship with him? Seen her sneak out one night? Broke into her phone and read the texts? Looked at their pictures?

Bile rose in her mouth at that thought.

If he'd seen some of those, he'd have definitely had reason to kill Duke. Especially given how freaked out he was about their age difference.

Duke hadn't been a predator. He'd been the one who tried to stop them from having a relationship. It had taken Hadley forever to convince him that everything would be fine.

But what if she'd been wrong? What if that was what got him killed?

Tears stung her eyes. She tried blinking them away, but it didn't do any good. They fell uncontrollably. She held her hand over her cheeks so nobody would see.

Was her dad capable of murder? He *did* have a temper. Or at least, he used to. He hadn't truly freaked out in years. Luna had probably never even seen their father lose all sense of control.

Hadley flashed back every time his brows began to furrow. She'd told the shrink that didn't happen anymore to get out of the stupid appointments. They had helped a little for a while. But they were mostly a waste. Focusing on her achievements was a much better use of time.

Usually.

It wasn't doing her any good today. She couldn't even practice.

She needed to talk to the detective.

If Dad did kill Duke, he needed to answer for it. Sure, he was her father. And she didn't want to see him go to jail.

But if he killed her boyfriend?

All bets were off. That was the ultimate betrayal. He could have talked with her. Gotten her side instead of flying off the handle and killing him with one of those overrated blue knives.

Then there was the question of *if* he'd done it. Neither of the people in Duke's house on Sunday night had been Dad. But they did mention him.

And they *had* walked to their house afterward.

Maybe Dad had paid someone to do it. That had to cost a ton, and they weren't exactly rolling in cash. They lived in a nice neighborhood, but they were far from rich.

Anything was possible. And who was there to defend Duke? Just the cops. Not his family, none of the people he worked with. She hadn't seen anyone step up. Nobody had come to his house.

Yeah, there'd been buzz online. Someone had set up a fundraiser. But that was it.

She needed to do something. At least tell the detective what she thought. Then the cops could look into it. If she was wrong, then Dad wouldn't be arrested. They'd just question him some more. He would be pissed for sure, but at least then the cops would have a starting point. Right now, it seemed like they had nothing.

And after her parents found out about those detectives questioning her at school, they weren't likely to approach her again.

This was all on her.

Her stomach threatened to spew her lunch all over the bleachers.

Even though part of her hated Dad for his temper, for ruining her childhood, another part of her wanted to protect him. He wasn't evil. He'd changed his ways, been a great dad lately. Mostly.

Unless he'd committed murder and covered it up.

If he'd killed Duke, he needed to pay. There was no getting around that.

Hadley got up and took shaky steps down the bleachers.

"Where you going, Morris?" bellowed the coach.

She put her hands on her stomach.

"That doesn't answer my question!"

Hadley glared at him. "I'm leaking!"

He waved her toward the locker room, his face turning green.

Why were men so squeamish about something so normal? She barely managed not to roll her eyes.

Some of the other girls giggled.

Hadley hurried back to her locker and stared at the detective's card. Her pulse drummed in her ears. Could she really do this? Turn her father in? Her own flesh and blood?

Duke's face flashed in her mind.

She *had* to do it. For him.

If Dad had done wrong, that was on him. He would have to face the consequences of his actions.

Besides, for all she knew, they were still looking at her since she'd made out with him in his car right before his murder. She could get falsely accused.

But what if her telling the police about Dad's weapons put him in the same position? Especially when he was probably innocent.

They both looked guilty.

There was only one way to get to the bottom of it all.

Hadley nearly dropped the card as it shook in her hand.

She pulled out her phone.

Instead of tapping in the number, she scrolled through the pictures she'd taken the night before. So many weapons. Including one of those curved knives on the wall — the kind that had supposedly killed Duke.

She dropped her phone in the locker and puked in a toilet.

After rinsing her mouth, she stared at her reflection. She was strong enough to do this. To tell the police everything she knew.

It was the only way to get justice for Duke.

Hadley glanced around to make sure she was alone. Then she called the detective.

Who said she'd be there in twenty minutes.

Exactly the time Hadley would be leaving practice.

After throwing up again, she changed into her regular clothes and watched the rest of practice.

Coach said nothing about her outfit.

As soon as he released them, Hadley fled to her locker and grabbed her things. Nearly crashed into the detective just outside the main doors.

"Miss Morris."

Hadley cleared her throat. "Detective."

"You have urgent information for me?"

She nodded and played with her ponytail, sure the woman could hear her thundering heart.

"Let's talk in the office again."

Hadley shook her head. "I don't want anyone over-hearing."

The detective lifted a brow. "You don't?"

"Can we talk over there?" She pointed to a bench under a tree with nobody near it.

"Or my car."

"No." The last thing Hadley needed was for kids to talk about her getting into a cop car. The rumors would leave out the part about her sitting in the front seat. "It's there, or I'm not telling you anything."

Annoyance flashed across the detective's face, but she quickly covered it with a forced smile. "Sure. Whatever makes you comfortable."

Nothing about this made her *comfortable*.

They made their way over, Hadley trudging behind. Second thoughts screamed at her. She ignored them. She was doing the right thing.

The detective sat at the middle of the bench, and

Hadley sat as close to the edge as possible. She stuck her hands in her pockets to hide their shaking.

"You found something?" Stewart took out her tablet.

Hadley drew in a deep breath. "Did you find anything on those people I told you about last time?"

"I can't discuss an ongoing investigation."

"But I can?"

"If you want to help us solve this case. Did you figure out where you were before he died?"

"It's like I told you — I was at my play! That's not why I'm here." She hesitated, seeing a group of cheerleaders heading their way.

"Continue." The detective's voice was like sandpaper.

"I … I don't know if this has anything to do with the murder."

"If you think you have something, give me the information, and my team will figure that out. That's our job."

Hadley twisted a strand of hair around her finger and sucked in a wavering breath. "Well, I found a bunch of swords and stuff in my dad's things."

Stewart's eyes widened, and her expression froze momentarily. "Swords?"

"Yeah. I didn't know he had those."

"Do you know what kind they are?"

"I don't know anything about swords. Just that I saw some with all of his stuff."

"When did you find them?" She made furious notes on her tablet.

Guilt stung. Maybe she was being a terrible daughter. But she was definitely being the girlfriend Duke needed when nobody else was on his side. "Last night."

"When your dad was out?"

Hadley jolted. "You know about that?"

"I spoke with him briefly."

"Last night?"

The woman nodded. "Can you explain to me what they look like?"

"The swords? I got a couple of pictures."

"Why didn't you say so?"

Hadley dug for her phone. "I wasn't thinking about it. You make me nervous."

Detective Stewart smiled. "Honey, if you haven't done anything, you have no reason to be nervous. I'm just trying to solve a murder."

And that could land her dad in jail. Her stomach lurched, but she managed to control her nerves this time. Once she felt in control of herself, she found the pictures. They were blurrier than they seemed last night when she'd been studying them in her room.

"Those are great," the detective reassured her. "Now, I need you to text them to me."

"Same number I called you on?"

"Yes." The detective made more notes, her cheeks flushing.

"Sent them." Hadley felt sick again. What kind of a daughter was she? Dad wasn't a bad guy. And if he went to jail, Luna would grow up without him.

Was she destroying her family?

"Got them. This is really going to help." The detective flipped through the pictures. "Where did you find these? Specifically."

"In his office at home."

"Were there any other weapons?"

"He has some in bags I didn't get to look at, and others displayed on the wall, but those are just for decoration."

The detective tilted her head. "Just *used* for decoration? Are they actual weapons?"

Hadley sighed. "They're real."

More notes.

"But that doesn't mean he killed Duke."

"No." Stewart shook her head emphatically. "You could actually be helping to eliminate your father as a suspect. What weapons did he have displayed?"

Knives. One the same kind the police were interested in.

Hadley swallowed. "Um, it's hard to remember."

"No pictures?"

"It was too dark."

The detective leaned closer. "Do you think you can get me any more photos?"

Hadley's heart leaped into her throat. "His office is locked. I don't know."

"You got in last night."

"Yeah."

"I need those pictures. Think you can do it again?"

Hadley played with a fingernail.

"Or are you afraid of what he'll do?"

She shook her head, her mouth going dry again.

"Do you feel safe at home?"

"Yes! And I need to get going." She rose. "Homework, you know."

"You'll send me those pictures."

"I'll try."

"One more question."

Hadley looked at her.

"Was one of those displayed weapons a Valderdorf knife, the kind that he sells?"

Her mouth fell open. No words would come.

"No need to answer." The detective smiled. "Thank you for everything."

Hadley tried to walk away but couldn't move.

What had she just done?

Chapter Twenty-Eight

BRAD HESITATED before opening the front door. All he wanted was to sneak upstairs and get some sleep. He and Faye had talked for hours about their relationship and how little he cared about Rose late into the night. They'd rehashed old issues, and she'd raised a few new ones.

He was drained. Slogging through work after only a few hours of sleep, stuck behind the counter selling knives most of the day. It kept Rose out of his hair, but he hadn't talked to Kurt.

That was probably his boss's plan. He'd only been around for a few hours and had managed to avoid Brad the entire time.

It was time to face the truth that Kurt wasn't going to help him.

Brad didn't know why his boss had shifted, but he had. He was on his own now — not only to keep the company out of the investigation but to watch out for himself. If he wanted an attorney, he needed to secure one of his own.

The thought of it all made every inch of his body ache. The pain was too much. Brad was used to being in control.

Never had he run into so much trouble when *he'd* killed someone. Rarely did the cops turn to him, and when they had, Kurt always had his back.

What changed?

Brad would have to look into that later. For now, he needed to sleep. Nothing could get between him and his bed. Or his office couch — that would be better. He could lock himself away from anyone needing him. They could wait until morning.

Brad closed his eyes and prepared himself to face his family. They would object to him hiding away for the night, but he would assure them everything was fine. Faye should understand. She had been up with him.

He pushed open the door and stepped inside, taking in the familiar sounds of conversation and TV. But there was one voice that didn't belong.

Allison.

Brad swore under his breath. Had Faye actually invited that woman inside? Even knowing how he felt about her? After their talk last night, were they really not on the same page yet?

He clenched his fists and counted to twenty. Perhaps there was a reasonable explanation. Maybe there was news about who had killed Duke. That had to be it.

He marched into the kitchen and gave his wife a kiss. Blatantly ignored their troublemaker of a neighbor, standing tall as he turned his back to her. "I'm going upstairs unless you need me."

"Lovely to see you, Brad," said Allison in a sing-song.

He furrowed his brows, still eyeing his wife. "Can I speak with you privately?"

Faye yawned. "I've got to check the chicken."

"I can watch it for you," Allison offered.

"Really, I've got it." Faye moved around Brad and pulled open the oven.

He turned toward her and accidentally made eye contact with Allison.

She smirked.

"What's your problem?" he demanded.

Faye glared at him. "Brad!"

He kept his focus on Allison. "I'm serious."

"What do you mean?"

"Stop feigning innocence."

Allison crossed her arms. "I'm not doing anything wrong."

"No? Why are you suddenly so friendly? You never came around before Duke was killed. This is the house to be at to get all the juicy gossip, right? And it's the perfect place to stir up some trouble. Do you enjoy trying to ruin marriages?"

Allison started to say something, but he cut her off. "I have news for you, lady. My marriage is strong. Faye and I have been together since we were teenagers, and we've faced things together that you can't even imagine. Trying to paint me as a cheater won't work. I'm faithful to my wife."

"Have you ever killed anyone?" She stepped closer, hands on her hips.

"I didn't kill Duke. Had no reason to."

"None?"

"Exactly. If you think I'm so shallow to kill someone over Christmas lights, you're insane."

"Brad!" Faye stepped between them. "This needs to stop. Luna's in the next room, and Zeke can probably hear it too."

He drew in a deep breath. "Luna's absorbed in her

cartoons as always, and Zeke is always wearing his headphones."

"He's doing homework."

"And he listens to music when doing that. Neither of them are listening to us."

She glowered at him.

Brad turned back to their guest. "You should leave now. And stay out of our lives."

"What about—" Allison stopped, staring at something behind him.

Brad whipped around.

Zeke trudged into the kitchen with a mopey expression.

"Everything okay?" Brad asked.

His son shrugged.

Faye rushed over. "Are you okay, sweetie? You look ill."

Brad put his hand on Zeke's forehead. No fever. "He's fine."

"I just want a snack."

"Do you need anything?" Allison asked. "I can run to the store for medicine."

"Weren't you just leaving?" Brad snapped.

Zeke ignored them both and opened the dishwasher.

Brad turned to Allison. "Be sure to tell Wes hi for me."

Her mouth formed a straight line.

Zeke turned to Brad. "Hey, Dad. Isn't this that Valder-dorf knife you were talking about?"

Brad's stomach sank.

Faye's face paled.

Allison's eyes lit up. "Is it the one the police asked about?"

"I told you to leave." Brad pointed toward the door.

She didn't budge. "Why's it in the dishwasher? To wash away evidence?"

His blood boiled. "We have several of those lying around. One we use for cooking." He spun around. "I don't know why I'm defending myself to you. You're leaving."

"I'm not going anywhere."

"Yes, you are. And don't come back. You're not welcome here."

"Do the police know about this knife?" Allison asked. "I bet that detective would love to hear about it."

"Get out!"

Everyone jumped at Brad's outburst.

"I'm serious. If I see you here again, I'm calling the cops."

"That's rich. But it's actually a good idea. The detective gave me her card. I think I'll go over there and give her a call."

Finally, Allison left.

But not without causing even more trouble than before.

Zeke's face fell. "Sorry, Dad."

Brad put his hand on his shoulder. "You didn't do anything wrong."

"I was just trying to help."

"Exactly."

"But now you're going to be in trouble, and it's my fault."

He shook his head. "We have nothing to worry about because I didn't kill Duke. Just because we have the same type of knife that was used in the crime doesn't mean I'm going to be arrested for something I didn't do. None of these knives have any of DNA on them."

"But now the cops are going to come back."

"Let them. I have nothing to hide."

Chapter Twenty-Nine

BRAD TOSSED his empty beer bottle into the recycle bin and glared at Faye. "How could you have let that woman into our house? Especially knowing how I feel about her?"

"She means well." She checked the temperature of the chicken.

"Yeah, if by meaning well, you're saying she's trying to destroy us."

"That's not fair."

"Isn't it? What about last night, making up a story about me and Rose?"

Zeke watched the argument, his head bouncing back and forth between them.

"Go finish your homework."

"Already did." The kid reached for a bag of chips.

"Don't ruin your dinner."

He glared at Brad.

"I'm serious. Your mom is putting a lot of work into it."

"I can eat both."

"Drop the chips and go to your room."

Zeke let the chips go, and the bag fell on the floor. He stormed out of the kitchen.

"Pick those up!"

Faye glanced at him. "You did tell him to drop them."

He threw his hands in the air. "I don't have time for this. You do realize that detective is coming here? And your *friend* is probably speaking to her right now, giddy at the thought of seeing me arrested."

"Like you said, we have nothing to worry about since we didn't do anything."

"Except the lie you told about our date."

"Your coworkers said they saw us."

"What if another helpful neighbor comes forward, swearing that they saw you at home? Or Duke coming over here? Or—"

"Okay. I get your point. But if there's no blood on the knife, they can't do anything."

"The knife that went through the *dishwasher*? Nothing suspicious about that."

"But it would still have DNA on it, wouldn't it? If it was a murder weapon?"

"They could say I soaked it in bleach. I'm sure they could come up with a dozen likely scenarios. No idea how I'd prove otherwise."

"I'm sure Kurt's lawyer will give you ideas."

"He's putting me off. I don't have access to his attorney."

"Why not?"

"You'd have to ask Kurt."

She held his gaze. "What are we going to do, then?"

"Good question."

"Is our alibi really a problem?"

"It sure as hell could become one."

She squeezed a dish towel before looking him in the eyes. "Where were you that night?"

"What?"

"You came home with that blood behind your ear. Where were you?"

"How many times do we have to go over this? I was at a convention. Some idiot cut himself with one of our knives."

"But how did it get behind your ear? That doesn't make sense to me."

He rubbed his temples. "People's idiocy doesn't make any sense to me, either, Faye. Let's focus on what's important."

"You're hiding something."

He stared at her in disbelief. "Is that what you really think?"

"I'm sure of it."

Guilt stabbed his chest. He'd always managed to keep this work a secret from his wife without lying about anything else.

"You can't even deny it." Anger flared in her eyes.

"I'm doing the best I can with a crappy situation! Do you have any idea the stress I'm under? Between the investigation and Kurt turning his back on me, plus the issue with Hadley — it's a wonder I'm holding it together at all. I'm not dealing with your accusations on top of everything else."

He stormed out of the kitchen and nearly tripped over Zeke in the hall. "Were you listening in?"

Zeke scrambled to his feet. "You should be nicer to Mom."

Faye came out of the kitchen. "You really should be."

"Neither one of you have any idea the pressure I'm under."

Zeke glared at him. "And you think that gives you the right to treat everyone else however you want? That's classic."

"Classic?" Brad exclaimed. "What are you talking about?"

His son breathed heavily. "You're always telling me to turn the other cheek, but then you just boss the rest of us around — especially when you're mad. What happens if I stand up to you?"

"Stand up to me? For what?" Brad looked back and forth between his wife and son. They were coming at him from every side. "Where is this coming from?"

"You never listen to me!" Zeke's face reddened. "Or follow your own advice. Because it doesn't work. Right?"

Brad took a moment to collect himself. "I want you to have a better life."

"By getting picked on at school? Because that's exactly what looking the other way does. It gets me picked on even more! You know what *does* work?"

"I'm going to guess standing up for yourself."

"Yes! And you know who taught me how to do that?"

"No idea."

Zeke's eyes narrowed. "Duke."

Brad stumbled back. "You too?"

"He was never too busy. Now he's gone." Zeke's mouth wobbled. "My mentor's gone."

"Your *mentor*?" Brad looked at Faye for help. "Did you know about this?"

She shook her head.

Brad leaned against the wall and rubbed his temples. "Why didn't you tell me? I would've helped."

"Duke noticed I was upset. He told me about when he was growing up and had to deal with a bully at school. I bet nobody's ever picked on you!"

Brad would've laughed at the absurdity of the accusation if he didn't feel like he'd completely failed his son. "I've been picked on plenty. You could've talked to me."

Zeke shook his head and fled upstairs.

"Did you know about this?"

Faye shook her head. "I—"

Brad trudged up the stairs, unable to deal with anything else. How had he managed to miss what his son was going through? And even worse, Zeke thought he couldn't relate.

Hadley stepped out of her room and glared at him.

His heart sunk. "What did I do?"

"You've been lying to us."

Now it was definitely coming from all sides. "About what?"

"You're going to pretend not to know what I'm talking about?"

"I have no clue what you're talking about."

"Forget it!" She returned to her bedroom and slammed the door.

He stared at the closed door and shook his head.

Everything was unraveling, and Brad didn't know what to do about any of it.

Chapter Thirty

BRAD HIT the snooze on his phone again. But it still wouldn't turn off.

Faye rolled over. "That's the doorbell."

"This early?" Brad groaned. "What kind of lunatic bothers people at this hour?"

"I don't know. Can you check?"

"Of course. That's what I do." He pulled on a pair of jeans and hurried down the stairs.

Ding-dong!

"I'm coming!"

He opened the door to see Detective Stewart and her sidekick standing on his porch.

"Do you realize what time it is?"

She didn't apologize. "We wanted to catch you before you left for work."

"Congratulations, you did it. What do you want?"

"We're here to collect your Valderdorf knives."

He stared at them, trying to make sense of what she said. "You want my knives?"

"The Valderdorfs," she clarified.

"I heard. Do you have a warrant?"

Then it hit him. Allison had called them.

Of course, she had.

Detective Stewart stepped forward. "It would be better for everyone if you hand them over without the warrant. We get a warrant, and we'll be going through your whole house. All we're asking for right now is your cooperation."

"And the knives," said the sidekick.

Fear raced through him at the thought of the police rifling through his office. Kurt's warning to keep the investigation away from BlueBlade danced through his mind. He drew a deep breath. "As you already seem to know, I have multiple Valderdorfs. I'll need a few minutes to gather them."

He stepped inside and started to close the door.

Stewart stepped forward. "We can wait inside."

"Or you can wait out here."

"For all your neighbors to see?"

Brad gritted his teeth. "Come inside."

He didn't offer them a seat before heading to the kitchen. The Valderdorf was still in the dishwasher. Good thing they didn't see that — not that it likely mattered, since Allison had probably told them all about it being there the night before. He thought about bagging it up, but why make Stewart's job easier? They would already expect his prints to be on the thing. And it wasn't like any of his knives had been used in the murder.

"Here you go." He forced a grin as he handed it to the detective. "The others are upstairs."

The officer stared at the curved blade. "This is a kitchen knife?"

"When you've worked at BlueBlade as long as I have, yes." Brad strolled up the stairs, trying to give the impression that he wasn't worked up over this.

He went into his office and took the dusty Valderdorf off the wall, leaving it on its display board. He looked around the room, trying to recall if he had any others in here.

One of his sword bags on the floor caught his attention — sticking out at an angle instead of pushed against the wall.

He always left them against the wall.

Someone had been in here.

Blood drained from his body. That meant someone had figured out his lock code.

Had that someone used one of his Valderdorfs to commit the murder?

It couldn't be the one in his hand. Not with all the dust. For once, he was grateful for his laziness. He always meant to clean the office later, which rarely came.

What if that knife in the dishwasher was the murder weapon?

Had someone in his family killed Duke with it and then put it in there in hopes of removing evidence?

Hopefully, they'd soaked it in bleach first.

He hated thinking that, but he'd rather his wife or kids had thought that far ahead rather than risk going to prison.

Not that there was time to think about that now. He needed to get his knives to the cops so they could leave. But first, he had to check the bag.

Everything looked in place. The bag was full of swords, so none were missing.

Could he have bumped the bag and not noticed? He *had* been under a lot of stress. And that was a much better thought than any of his family members breaking in here and killing the guy next door.

Brad picked back up his knife and looked around,

trying to remember if he had another Valderdorf in the room.

No, he didn't. They didn't use the company's weapons on their marks. It was too dangerous.

He left the office and quickly changed his lock code.

Hadley entered the hall, rubbing her eyes. "What's going on with the doorbell so early?"

Brad held up the knife. "The police are here to collect all of our Valderdorfs."

Her eyes widened.

"Go back to bed." He headed for his bedroom, where he had two older knives sealed in boxes to maintain their value. So much for that if the idiot police opened them.

Hadley was still standing in the hall when he returned, juggling everything.

"Aren't you going back to bed?"

"You aren't in trouble, are you?"

"No, because I didn't kill Duke. These will prove it."

She swallowed, gave him an apologetic look, then disappeared into her room.

Brad made his way downstairs and handed off his prized Valderdorfs. "As you can see, two are sealed. They're an older model and worth far more unopened. I'd appreciate it if you keep them that way."

Stewart arched a brow. "You sure they're factory sealed?"

"Of course they are. Why would I open a collector's item? When will I get these back?"

"When we're done with them. Thank you for your cooperation."

Brad grumbled as he let them out.

Of course, they were going to open the boxes.

By the time he returned to his room, his alarm was

actually going off. He turned it off and slunk on the bed. It was already the perfect day to call in sick.

"They took all the Valderdorfs?" Faye asked.

He nodded, deep in thought. "We need to find out everything we can about the kids' involvement with Duke. Probably should find out if Luna is hiding anything about him, too."

"Luna?" Faye exclaimed. "Would you listen to yourself?"

"Think about it. Everyone else in this house has been hiding something about Duke. It makes sense that she would, too."

"She's seven!"

"Did you expect our seventeen-year-old and our four-teen-year-old to have secret relationships with him?"

She frowned. "No."

"Exactly."

"Looks like we all have something in common — except that you aren't coming clean."

He stared at her. "About what?"

"The blood behind your ear!"

He would never miss a spot of blood again. How could such a stupid oversight lead to his undoing?

"Well?" Faye looked at him expectantly.

His mind raced. "Rose and I were—"

"Rose? What were you doing with her?" Faye scowled. "You said everything was platonic!"

"If you'd let me finish what I was saying—"

Ding-dong!

He swore.

Ding-dong!

Faye looked at her phone's screen. "It's the cops again."

"Of course it is."

"What were you going to say about Rose? What were you two doing together?"

Ding-dong!

"I'll tell you after I get rid of them." He hurried downstairs.

there were no forgoing or say about [illegible] "That work on two long journey.

Faye say

She [illegible] after [illegible] go of [illegible] far too much thought.

Chapter Thirty-One

By the time Faye got downstairs, the cops were already inside.

"What's going on?" she asked.

The detective looked at her. "Our testing kit found blood on one of the knives."

"Do you know if it's human?" Brad demanded.

"We'll be the ones asking questions." Detective Stewart glared at him. "You'll need to come down to the station for questioning."

Faye ran to Brad's side, her heart hammering. "Is he under arrest?"

"Not yet."

"Then question him here."

"We need him down at the station."

Her mind raced. "But you already know we were on a date. His coworkers saw us. He couldn't have done it!"

The officer stepped forward. "We've heard a conflicting story that we need to look into."

She and Brad exchanged worried looks.

"From whom?" she asked. "What did they say?"

And did it have anything to do with what Brad was about to say upstairs? He had started to say he'd been doing something with Rose.

The woman whose lipstick had been on his face at the bar. The woman who had been hanging on him at the Super Bowl party. Whispering in his ear. She'd managed to get him to eat sushi when he'd refused to try it with Faye for years.

"We'll be the ones asking questions," Detective Stewart repeated.

Faye turned to her husband. "What about—?"

Stewart stood between them. "Do you wish to change your story, ma'am?"

Her mind went blank. What did the cops know? Was it something about Brad, or had someone seen Duke come over right before being killed?

Could she be a suspect instead of Brad? Or what about Hadley? Did they know she'd been seeing him? Or did Rose somehow play into this? Maybe Brad found out about Hadley and Duke, then talked his lover into killing him?

She choked on the thought. Pleaded with her eyes for a response from Brad. "Rose—"

The detective cleared her throat and stepped between them, looking at Faye. "A neighbor saw you talking with Duke the night he was killed."

Brad's mouth fell open. "Faye won't even harm a spider!"

The detective looked at Brad. "So, you admit that you two weren't on a date?"

"I was covering for her," he admitted. "Faye is innocent, but I knew that it looked bad, her seeing him so close to the time of death."

"You'd have been better off with the truth, Mr.

Morris."

He nodded. "I realize that now."

"We're going to have to take you both in to the station."

"Neither of us is guilty. Faye never left the house that night. Our house cameras can prove it. Duke came, he left, but Faye stayed here. I've seen the footage."

"Why lie?"

"To protect her!" Spittle flew from his mouth.

"What about *you*? We've got your bloody knife and plenty of people who think you had more than enough reason to kill the man. So where were you?"

"I *was* out of town."

"And we should believe you why?"

Brad tugged on his hair.

Faye wanted to jump to his defense, but at the same time, she wanted to know where her husband had been. Besides "getting bloody at a convention."

Stewart glared at him. "Are you going to come willingly or not? We need you to explain the blood on—"

"If I can prove I wasn't even in town at the time, will you leave? You're probably going to find cow blood on that knife. We had roast beef a week ago. There's zero chance that even a drop of that blood belongs to Duke."

Faye's breath hitched. Where was he going with this? Had he been with Rose? Lying to Faye all this time?

He turned to her, clearly trying to communicate with his eyes, but she couldn't tell what her husband wanted to say.

"You weren't on a date with your wife?" Stewart traded a look with the officer.

Faye studied Brad.

His expression was a brick wall.

"Brad?" Her voice wavered.

"You killed Duke, didn't you?" asked the detective, staring him down.

His hands shook, but the rest of him remained steady. He glanced to Faye and mouthed *I love you* before turning to Stewart. "I couldn't have killed Duke because I was with Rose."

Faye gasped and clutched her heart. The world seemed to crumble around her.

He *had* been having an affair.

And she'd been stupid enough to believe his lies. She tried to speak. Nothing would come. There was no air in her lungs.

Brad dug into his pocket and pulled out his wallet. Handed a receipt to Stewart. "Here's your proof. Two desserts purchased at La Isla's" —he turned to Faye, widening his eyes — "near the Space Needle. I was in Seattle. Check the date and time. No way I could've killed that bastard."

"Bastard?"

"No, I *didn't* like him. Not one bit — but I never did anything to harm him. Nothing!" He gave Faye a pleading expression, but she turned away, unable to look at him.

In fact, she couldn't face anyone.

She ran upstairs and locked the bedroom door.

Chapter Thirty-Two

Brad had barely locked the front door before he bolted upstairs to their bedroom. He banged on the locked door. "Faye! We need to talk!"

No response.

"I know you're in there! You need to hear me out!"

"Go away!"

He pounded again. "Please!"

Nothing.

Brad swore. "You need to hear the truth!"

"I've heard enough. Leave me alone!"

He knocked some more until he finally surrendered. When she was like this, it was best to just give her time to think. Then he could explain himself. Or maybe she would assemble all of the pieces to reach the truth herself.

Or maybe she would never hear him out.

Brad looked in Luna's room. Empty. Probably watching cartoons downstairs. He found Hadley in the bathroom, straightening her hair.

She started to close the door.

But he blocked it with his foot. "I need to know every-thing about your relationship with Duke."

Her face reddened. "You don't *want* to know everything."

Brad hesitated. "You know what I mean."

"Not really." She set her flat iron on the sink. "What's going on? Why were you yelling at Mom?"

"I wasn't yelling. I was talking through a closed door."

"Whatever." Hadley began to apply her mascara.

"Was Duke good to you?"

"The best."

"He never hurt you?"

"No."

"You never had any reason to want to hurt him? Or worse?"

She spun around, tears shining in her eyes. "Stop!"

"I need to know."

"He never did anything bad to me. And I would never hurt him. I didn't kill him, so you need to stop implying that—"

"Do you have any idea who did?"

"The only person that makes any sense is *you.*"

Brad stumbled back. "Me?"

Her eyes narrowed. "Who else? He was always upstaging you, and you *have* to be number one. If you found out about him and me, that's serious motive."

"You think I could kill him?"

"Didn't you say you'd kill him yourself if he was alive?"

He blinked a few times. Hadn't he said to that Faye in private?

Hadley turned her back to him, still applying her makeup. "Why are you trying to pin this on me?"

"I'm not."

"Then leave me alone. His death has destroyed me. If I had any idea who did it, I would have told the police."

He froze. "What *did* you tell them?"

"Not much."

"Do they know about your relationship with him?"

"Dad, go away."

"I need to know!"

"Let them do their job. You should be worried about Mom." She closed the door, and the lock clicked.

He found Zeke downstairs, scarfing down a brightly colored cereal.

"Everything okay?" Zeke asked.

"How close were you to Duke?"

"You aren't going to yell at me again, are you?"

"I didn't yell at you before."

Zeke gave him a knowing look before shoving a spoonful in his mouth.

"Look, the police aren't getting anywhere. They're focused on me, but I didn't do it. If you know *anything*, I really need you to tell me."

Zeke sighed. "I just talked to him about bullies once in a while. Wasn't like it was every day or anything."

"He never mentioned anything about bullies that he might be dealing with?"

His son looked deep in thought for a moment. "He had some online trolls harassing him. Kids from when he was in middle school. But that was it. He definitely never said anything about someone wanting to kill him."

Brad frowned. His whole family knew Duke better than they'd let on, but none of them knew enough to point him toward the killer.

He could only hope the receipt to the dessert place would be enough to keep the detective away from him.

Looking into it, they would likely discover that he bought the two desserts alone and left with them.

Not that the alibi would even help, seeing as Brad was killing someone else while Duke was sucking on his final few breaths.

And Kurt wasn't helping.

He was screwed if he didn't find the real killer. This was all on him.

"I'm telling the truth," Zeke said.

Brad blinked a few times. He'd been so lost in thought he'd forgotten where he was. "Okay. If you do think of anything, let me know right away."

"Sure."

Brad needed to find out if Luna knew anything. Given the way things were going, he wouldn't have been surprised if she did. He went to the living room, but she wasn't there, and the TV was off. He returned to the kitchen. "Have you seen Luna?"

Zeke shook his head.

Brad hurried up the stairs. Her bedroom was empty. She wasn't in the playroom. Or anywhere upstairs.

He knocked on his bedroom door. "Is Luna in there?"

"No."

"Do you know where she is?"

"Did you check the front room?"

The one place he hadn't looked. "No."

Brad hurried downstairs, trying to imagine what kind of friendship his seven-year-old could have possibly struck up with Duke.

The front room was empty.

He hurried through the downstairs, checking every-where, including the laundry room.

Then he re-checked all the rooms upstairs. Looked in

all the closets and her favorite hiding spots when they played hide-and-seek.

But Luna was nowhere.

Had she gone outside?

The backyard was empty, including her hiding places. So was the front yard, but she knew better than to go out there alone.

Brad's heart threatened to explode.

His daughter was gone.

Chapter Thirty-Three

BRAD'S PHONE buzzed with a text. Relief washed through him with hope that it might be Luna. Then he realized what a stupid thought that was. His youngest child didn't even have a phone.

The message was from Rose: *Come next door. Luna's here. Enter through the back.*

He stared at the message in disbelief.

She's with you?

Hurry!

Brad slid the phone into his pocket and raced outside, almost forgetting to type in the alarm code before opening the door. He raced to his neighbor's, starting for the front before remembering that Rose had ordered him in through the back.

Maybe she'd discovered something about the killer. Though really, the only thing he cared about was bringing Luna back home. He'd nearly had a heart attack at the thought of her disappearing. Thank goodness she was just with Rose.

He fiddled with the latch, then opened the gate and found his way to the back door.

Unlocked.

Brad stepped inside. "Hello? Rose?"

"In here."

He hurried through the living room to the kitchen.

Rose sat at the table, sipping a mug with Duke's MLM company logo.

"Where's Luna?"

"She's fine. Sit." Rose nudged the seat across from her.

"I need to get my daughter."

Rose slammed the cup down. "I said *sit*."

"What the hell?" Brad looked around and called out, "Luna?"

"She's upstairs. Now sit!"

Brad ignored her and headed for the stairs. "Luna?"

"Daddy?" His little girl's voice sounded tiny, thin, and far away.

"Come down here, honey."

Rose stepped in front of him, blocking the way. "She's a little tied up at the moment. Sit."

"Excuse me?"

"Daddy!"

Brad darted around Rose.

She pulled out a Valderdorf. "I wouldn't do that."

He skidded to a stop. "What are you doing?"

"What should've been done on Friday."

The blood drained from his skull. "Friday?"

Her brows furrowed. "If I'd been the one to jump you, you'd have never gotten away. Instead, I had to kill your loser neighbor."

The room spun around him as pieces fell into place. "You framed me for Duke's murder?"

"Damn straight." She held the curved blade toward his neck. "Now *sit*."

"Are you okay, Luna?" he called.

"Help me, Daddy!"

Brad's heart shattered into a million pieces. He shoved Rose aside and lunged for the stairs.

She shoved the knife to his throat. Pain pricked where it pierced his flesh. "If you don't follow directions, you both die."

He turned around. Felt his neck. A speck of blood stained his finger.

"Now, Bradley."

He reached for his pocketknife.

"Not so fast!" Rose jammed her blade back to his throat. "Hand everything over."

"What?"

"Now!"

"Sure. Let's talk about this. I'm sure we can reach an agreement." He dug into his pocket and whipped out his knife, flipping it, so the blade sprang out. It wasn't nearly as impressive as her Valderdorf, but it was all he had. That and brute strength.

She'd made a mistake turning on him.

Rose blocked his arm. "Put it down."

"Ladies first." He nodded toward her weapon.

"You're such a chauvinist. I've always hated that about you." Her face contorted in disgust.

"What? No, I'm not."

"And you're blind to it. That's even worse."

He studied her. "What are you talking about?"

She hit his arms with shocking force.

His fingers lost their grip and sent his knife flying.

"Empty your pockets!" She forced her blade against his Adam's apple.

Brad cleared his throat and pulled out his wallet, phone, and another knife. He set each item on the counter, careful to put his phone facedown.

She sneered at him. "You're really prepared, aren't you?"

"You'd better not hurt Luna."

"I'd rather not, but that's up to *you*. Sit."

He shot her a death glare but did as he was told.

She took a seat across from him. Then stared him down.

"What do you want?"

"You dead."

"Why?"

Rose pressed her palms on the table and leaned forward. "I'm sick of being under your thumb. You're not even the boss, but I have to follow all of your stupid protocols. I should be a free agent by now, but you're always getting in the way of that."

"*My* protocols? Hello. The *company* has rules. We can't run around like rogue agents. The things you want to do—"

"Shut up!" She picked up the Valderdorf and thrust it toward him.

Brad gritted his teeth.

"I can't move up, and it's all your fault! You're always telling Kurt when I don't do things the way you want — like we're on a kindergarten playground. If it weren't for you, I could enjoy my targets more. Really make them pay! But *no*, I have to play by Brad's rules. Kill the bastards quickly. Never give them time to think and regret. Just off them. So humane, right?"

"Would you listen to yourself? You're insane."

"Me?" she scoffed. "What about you?"

"I follow the rules. It's taken me years to reach my rank. You think you can do it in months. You're—"

"Enough!"

"What do you want?"

"I already told you!" She leaped out of her chair and began to pace the room.

His pulse drummed in his ears. He watched for an opportunity to overpower her.

But her gaze never left him.

"We can talk about this … If you want more freedom in the company, let's come up with something together. We can go to the office and talk to Kurt. I'll back you up. How's that sound?"

"Don't patronize me!" Her nostrils flared.

"I'm trying to *help*. That's all I've ever done."

She spat on him. "Liar! You're a typical man — trying to push down the women. I *hate* you just as much as every other man I've had the pleasure to—"

"Let my daughter go, and you can do anything you want to me."

"Let her go so she can run home and call the cops? Nice try."

"She'll tell Faye I'm with you. My wife already thinks we're having an affair."

Rose smirked. "I'm still not sending that brat away."

"She's no brat!" Brad lunged for her.

But she blocked his swing and shoved him down. "Stay there!"

"No. If you're going to hurt me, I don't want Luna seeing it. It'll scar her for life."

"Good!" She punched him across the face.

He held his aching jaw. "You'd destroy a little girl?"

"Why not? Then maybe she'll grow up tough like me."

Brad glowered at her through narrowed eyes. "You're evil."

She got in his face. "And you're a dead man."

"Just let her go."

"She'll be fine. Like I said, she's tied up. Can't sneak down to see what I'm about to do to you."

His pulse was on fire as he turned toward the stairs and bellowed, "Luna! How'd you get there? GO BACK!"

Rose's eyes widened, and she whipped around toward the empty staircase.

But then, as she turned back to Brad, he wrapped his arms around her throat in a chokehold and squeezed.

She gagged and struggled against him. Kicked, flailed her arms. Sliced his shirt with the curved blade.

Agony shot through his arm, and blood trickled down to his wrist. But after a moment, the gash began to tingle and turn numb. His grip slipped.

He pulled away from her before she could turn and stab him again. "Did you put something on the knife?"

Rose leaped for him, covered his mouth and nose, then shoved his chest into the counter, bringing the knife back to his neck.

His vision blurred. He struggled to breathe, to push her off. Managed to pull away from the counter. Gasped for air.

She forced the blade to his throat yet again. Led him to the chair. Shoved him down.

Pulled out a gun. "I didn't want it to come down to this. Stay there and shut up!"

It took all of his self-control not to say anything.

The pistol was hers, not company-issued. So using it on him would tie the crime to her.

Rose pointed it at his head and grabbed a rope from an empty chair. Wrapped it around him, anchoring the other end with her foot, keeping the gun in place until she tied him up.

He couldn't move an inch. Not surprising, since Brad had been the one to train her. "What now?"

"I told you to shut it!" She waved the pistol around like a maniac.

His mind kept racing. There had to be something he could say to talk her down.

"I've been waiting so long for this day." She stopped pacing and waving her weapons to get in his face. "I'm going to take this nice and slow. You're going to suffer for everything you've ever done to me!"

"For training you to be the best?"

"Second best." She struck him with the gun.

He winced, his cheek throbbing.

Blue and red lights flashed on the ceiling.

Brad breathed a sigh of relief and tried to keep his expression from showing any emotion.

Rose turned back to him. "How should we start the games? I've dreamed of slicing your smug face to pieces. Watching the flesh hang down while you beg for mercy."

"You're one twisted—"

"I told you to shut up!" she spat at him again. "Actually, I'm going to wait for the face shredding. You can think about that while I work up to it."

The front door burst open.

Several uniformed officers stormed in, followed by Detective Stewart.

Rose's mouth dropped open. "What the ...?"

The detective marched over to Rose with handcuffs. "Rose Flores, you're under arrest for the murder of Duke Hill." She looked around. "And whatever's going on here."

"Attempted murder and kidnapping!" Brad told the detective. "My daughter is upstairs."

A blur of activity ensued as Rose resisted arrest and Stewart struggled to untie the rope.

"How did you know she killed Duke?"

"You mean given your lie about her being with you at the time of the murder?" Detective Stewart lifted a brow.

"That wasn't what I was referring to."

"I followed all the leads to her. The murder weapon was found in her car down the road — missing the exact piece of the blade left behind at Duke's murder. That's all I can tell you."

The rope came loose.

Brad jumped to his feet and headed for the stairs. "Luna!"

Stewart stopped him. "Two of my officers are getting her as we speak. We need to get you checked out by the medics outside."

"I'm *fine*. I want to see my daughter."

"At the ambulance. Come with me, Mr. Morris."

He grumbled but went along with her.

No surprise, his neighbors were gathered outside.

"I knew you were innocent all along!" Lucas yelled.

"Of course, your feud with Duke was friendly." Donna Brown gave him an exaggerated wave.

A pair of officers stepped outside with Luna. Not a mark on her.

Brad pulled away from the detective and drew his daughter into an embrace that he wanted to hold forever.

Chapter Thirty-Four

A WIDE ARRAY of emotions tore through Faye's psyche. Sympathy for Brad's wounds. Relief that he and Luna were okay. Shock that his mistress had been the one to kill Duke. Blinding rage that he had a mistress.

"Please, Faye, hear me out." He pleaded with his eyes.

"I've heard more than enough."

"There was never anything between Rose and me."

Faye turned toward Hadley and Zeke. "Watch cartoons with Luna."

"Both of us?" Hadley frowned.

"Yes." Faye gave her a look that told Hadley not to mess with her.

Hadley and Zeke took Luna to the living room.

Faye glared at her husband. "Make this quick."

"Upstairs."

"Don't want the kids hearing about your indiscretions?"

"There weren't any. But yes, they shouldn't hear what I have to say."

"Fine." Faye marched up to their room ahead of him, her stomach doing somersaults.

He closed and locked the door. Turned to her. "I lied about the affair to the police to cover for what I was really doing when Duke was murdered."

Faye folded her arms and tried to keep all the warring emotions out of her expression. "Cheating on me."

Brad shook his head. "You'd better sit down."

"I'll stand, thanks."

He held her gaze, stepped forward, and took her hand in his.

She snapped it away from his hold. Stepped back and glared at him. Heart pounded almost too loudly to hear him. "You don't get to touch me."

Brad didn't blink. "I'm an assassin, Faye. BlueBlade is a cover."

"What?" It felt as if all the blood had been drained from her body. She had to have heard him wrong. "It sounded like you said you're an assassin."

His expression softened. "I was killing a man named Juan Sanchez in Issaquah. It got messy because I was jumped — that's never happened before. So that's how I ended up with blood behind my ear Friday night. I was taking care of a man who tortured and killed children but had thus far evaded the police."

"You … you kill people?" She couldn't be hearing him right.

"We're a secret organization that goes after people who can't be caught through proper legal channels." He stepped toward her.

She backed up, shaking her head, studying the man she'd given her life to. "This can't be right. You're not a murderer."

"I'm not." He shook his head. "I only take out people

who are menacing society. The authorities can't get to them through the law, and we have government permission to do what's necessary. We keep people safe by eliminating actual murderers from the population. Not people like Duke — I would never have hurt him."

Her knees wobbled. She collapsed onto the bed. "You said you'd kill him when Hadley—"

"That was just talk. I *felt* like that, but no, I wouldn't kill him unless BlueBlade assigned him as a target. But even then, I wouldn't take anything so close to home. In fact, in Issaquah the other night, that was much closer than usual. I prefer to travel out of the area."

"To kill people." She swallowed, her throat dry.

He sat next to Faye and took her hand.

She didn't have the strength to pull away from his grasp.

"I've only ever killed anyone as part of my job. Faye, I'm one of the good guys. I swear it." His eyes seemed to be telling the truth.

"You've been lying to me all this time."

His face fell. "*Only* about work. I never lie about anything else to any of you. Ever."

Tears blurred her vision. "I don't know you at all."

"You know me better than anyone."

She shook her head, a tear spilling onto her cheek.

He wiped it away, his touch gentle. With hands that had killed. Many times.

Faye choked on air. "How can you do it?"

"For you, for the kids." He kissed another tear away. "The world would be a much more dangerous place without teams like ours."

Her stomach lurched, churned acid.

"The law can only do so much — it doesn't accomplish

nearly what it should. I shudder to think of what society would be like without—"

"All of your coworkers, too? They're all killers?"

"Some of them." He nodded. "Some only work in the shop and don't know anything. BlueBlade *is* a legitimate business. We go to conventions and other events, but not nearly as often as I've led you to believe."

She studied him again, trying to see the teenage boy she fell in love with. "How'd you get involved? When?"

"After the economy crashed and my real estate business fell apart."

"I know when you started working for BlueBlade. Did you know about the assassination business right away, or were you just selling knives and then found out about the rest?"

Brad took a deep breath. "Kurt knew how obsessed I was with finding my dad's murderer. He knew how it was eating away at me — at us. What I was doing to us. How my temper was spiraling out of control. He thought this would give me something to focus my energy on."

"Killing people."

"He was right. Killing criminals who evaded justice has helped to fill my need to get justice for Dad. No, I still don't know who killed him, but I'm doing good for other families who need the closure."

"You're a killer." She pulled away from him and grabbed a fistful of bedding.

"An assassin. And meanwhile, I've been able to keep looking into my dad's murder. It's given me time and resources I would never have had otherwise."

She closed her eyes and took several deep breaths, trying to make sense of it. "You've been killing people for over a decade?"

"Yes. But not just random people—"

"*Criminals.*"

"Right." He squeezed her hand.

She looked at him again. "I don't believe it. You couldn't kill anyone."

"Not in cold blood, no. But I've been trained to take down hardened killers and abusers. People who enjoy torturing others, destroying lives. I've taken out plenty of child killers and traffickers. Serial rapists. Murderers."

Faye ran her hands through her hair, gasped for air. "This can't be happening."

He kissed another tear as it trailed down her face. "I never wanted to hurt you. That's why I've kept this from you — *only this*." He shook his head as he shuddered. "But I can't have you thinking I was sleeping with Rose. I've *never* been unfaithful to you. Staying honest about everything other than work is a promise I made to myself from the start. I'd managed to keep that vow until Friday night, when you found the blood on me. Things got tricky. But I wanted to keep you out of it."

She shook her head. How could he be telling her this?

"Because of our lie to the police and their focus on me, things got sticky fast. Especially after finding out that Hadley and Zeke had their secrets with Duke—"

"I have to tell you something." Faye sat up straight, surprised that she wasn't nervous.

"What?" Brad asked, scooting closer to her.

"I didn't just cut Duke's hair that one time."

"Meaning?"

"He came to the salon for haircuts every other week. Always to me."

"Why?" Brad asked without even blinking.

"What was I supposed to do? Turn him away? Say that my husband wouldn't let me cut his hair? Do you know how ridiculous that would make me look to my colleagues?"

He sucked in his lips and nodded. "I understand. Now that you put it that way, I can see how unreasonable I was. It was only a haircut."

"And I'm the top stylist in the salon. I should have my own studio, not be working for someone else."

"I know you're the best," Brad acknowledged with a nod.

"Is your ... work ... the reason you don't want me having a salon here?"

"Right. I can't risk people snooping around. Someone could use your business as a way to get into my office when I'm not here to—"

"If you'd have given me a say in that, we could've come up with a solution."

"I realize that now."

Faye lay down and closed her eyes, her mind swimming with the fresh information and what it meant for not only their past but also their future. She tried to make sense of it all. "What was that receipt you gave the police? For the date you took with Rose?"

"You mean the date I lied about to cover for you since the police knew you were here." He leaned back and took her hand again, rubbing shapes on her palm. "That was for the dessert I picked up for you Friday night. It was *you* I was thinking about."

"After killing a man."

"After my assignment."

"What made that night different?"

A few beats passed before he answered. "I suppose being jumped gave me a new perspective on everything. My life flashing before my eyes — if that's not too dramatic. I realized we'd been drifting apart, and I wanted to bring your favorite dessert home to show you how much I still care."

My husband, the romantic assassin. She rubbed her eyes. "You're going to have to give me time to process … I'm not sure I'll ever be able to believe this … not really."

"The fact that I've kept this from you or that I'm a trained assassin?"

"All of it."

"It was only to protect you. The less you know—"

She sat up, her heart fluttering. "Wait a minute."

"What?"

Worry shot through her. "What if Rose implicates you now that she's been arrested? You'll go to jail."

He shook his head. "Neither Kurt nor his father would ever allow that to happen."

"I don't understand."

"They have records of *everything*. Kurt could drop her files into the hands of the prosecuting attorney, and she would never see daylight again."

"What do you mean by everything? Is there more? Other than the assassinations? How could Kurt keep her from talking — would they threaten her family?" Her heart clenched at the idea of someone threatening Hadley, or Luna, or Zeke. "Would your bosses ever hurt me or the kids if—"

Brad squeezed her hands and looked into her eyes. "You're all safe. I would *never* let anything happen to you."

"But if—"

"But nothing. You four are untouchable. Rose won't drag me into this. The fate she'd meet would be worse than death, worse than prison. Same for me if I was ever foolish enough to loosen my lips. She isn't going to talk."

"I have another question."

Brad nodded for her to continue.

"Our trip to the Caribbean. I woke up that one night to an empty bed and couldn't reach you or find you anywhere. I'd never been so scared in my life. You had a crappy excuse about helping that scuba diver repair a hole in his boat. But when I looked the next day, his boat seemed fine. It hadn't been touched. You insisted you two had done such a good job it was like new. Is this what *that* was about?"

His expression tightened. "Yes. Kurt was supposed to leave me alone. It was a family vacation, but the jerk called and demanded I take care of a guy they found hiding a few towns over from where we were. I didn't have any of my weapons — can you imagine me trying to get those past customs? — but I was expected to execute the job anyway.

A lump formed in her throat. "I thought you were hooking up with Jessica again."

"There is no *again*. I never touched the woman! We talked and got a little too close emotionally. But I cut all ties after I realized my mistake." He drew a deep breath and pulled Faye into his arms. She could hear his heart pounding. "If you ever suspect me of seeing someone else, know that it's a cover for something else. Just like earlier, when I told the cops I was with her — it was for you. I love *you*. It's only ever been you."

"Jessica wasn't in the Caribbean?"

"I never saw her if she was. I only lied to cover an assassination. And now I turn off my phone while on vacation. Kurt hasn't been able to reach me during our family time since."

Faye looked deeply into his eyes and rested her head against his. "How do you do it?"

"What do you mean?"

"Kill people. Live with it."

"I focus on the greater good. The lives being saved by taking these people out of the picture. The justice system is flawed, so the world needs people like us."

She shook her head. "I'm not sure I'll ever be able to understand."

Brad laced his fingers through hers. "I don't expect you to … just promise you'll believe in my motives. That everything I do is for you and the children. To give you all the safest world possible."

Faye nodded. "That much I do believe."

Chapter Thirty-Five

BRAD FINISHED his beer and turned to Larry. "Is it just me, or is this show ridiculous?"

His older neighbor chuckled. "I don't get it either, but Sue loves the Academy Awards."

Brad looked around his full living room. Half the guests were gathered around the screen. "I don't understand the draw."

Larry shrugged. "It's a good excuse for everyone to get together. And under happier circumstances. Duke's murderer is in jail, and our neighborhood is safe again." He leaned closer and whispered, "Do you know why your coworker did it?"

"I'm guessing it was a lover's quarrel. I didn't realize they had been seeing each other, but evidence has come to light that he was trying to break things off. Seems she didn't like that idea."

Larry shook his head in disbelief. "Young people these days. Whatever happened to nursing a heartache and moving on? Did you hear about that man in Seattle who killed his wife and kids because he wanted out of the marriage? It's like people don't know what divorce is anymore."

"I don't get it, either." Brad opened another beer and took a long sip.

Half the people cheered at the TV.

"Did the right team score?" Larry snickered.

"You'd think."

Faye came over. "Sorry to interrupt, but have either of you seen Allison?"

Brad shook his head. "No, thankfully."

She scowled at him before turning to Larry. "Have you?"

"No. Maybe she went home to rest. I noticed she kept rubbing her belly and eyes earlier. I remember when Sue was pregnant, it seemed like she needed three times the sleep."

Faye frowned. "She went home to grab some sugar and eggs for cookies, but she said she felt fine."

Brad patted his wife on her shoulder. "I'll bet she decided to make the cookies at home. Last I looked, our oven was stuffed."

"I tried calling her. I'm starting to worry."

Brad glanced over at Wes, who was roaring with laughter at something one of the millennials had said. "Maybe she told her husband what's going on."

Faye shook her head. "I already asked him. He hasn't heard anything."

"He's obviously not worried. Maybe you shouldn't be, either."

"I'm going to check on her."

"You stay here. I'll send him to check on his wife."

"Are you sure?"

Brad stood, and without a word, marched over to Wes.

"What do you want?" Wes asked.

"My wife is worried about Allison. Did you know she's been gone a while?"

Wes shrugged. "Went to get stuff for cookies or something."

"In the dark, pregnant."

"This is a safe neighborhood."

Lane leaped up and pulled on Cassidy's arm. "We'll go check on her. There's something at our place I want to grab anyway."

"Thank you." Brad glared at Wes, who was already back to laughing with the other guests.

He returned to his seat with Larry.

"Such a class act." Larry gestured toward Wes.

"You heard that?"

"He's loud when drunk."

"And a jerk." Brad thought back to Wes calling Allison from the bar to tattle on Brad. "Definitely a jerk when alcohol's involved."

The subject changed to sports until a little while later when a commotion sounded from the front entry.

Brad hurried over to find out what was happening.

Cassidy leaned against the door frame, her skin ashen.

Faye covered her mouth with both hands, her eyes shining with tears.

Brad hurried over and pulled her close. "What's the matter?"

She clung to him. "Allison's dead."

He gave her a double-take. "What?"

"It's true." Cassidy's voice wobbled. "Lane and I saw her lying in a pool of blood! She's dead."

Faye pressed her face against Brad's chest. "Who could murder a pregnant woman?"

"She wasn't pregnant," Cassidy said.

Everyone spoke at once.

Cassidy held up a hand and waited for silence. "The fake belly was lying beside her, ripped to shreds."

"Someone needs to call the cops." Brad pulled out his phone.

"Lane did. She's there, waiting. I came to tell you guys."

Wes appeared. "What's going on?"

Cassidy collapsed into sobs.

"What is it?" Wes demanded.

Nobody spoke. Brad didn't want to be the one to break the news, and it didn't look like anyone else did, either.

The color drained from Wes's face. He burst into a run, tearing outside.

Donna Brown turned to Brad. "So. Another person you can't stand is dead."

Everyone turned to look at him.

His stomach dissolved into acid. "I was here the whole time! You all saw me."

"I didn't," Donna said.

Brad had spent most of the evening talking with Larry. But looking around to find his friend, a terrible realization settled into his bones.

Someone was going after him.

One murder might be a coincidence, but two couldn't be.

Especially with Rose behind bars.

This was personal.

A Quick Favor...

If you enjoyed this book, please take a moment to write a short review on your favorite online bookstore so other readers can enjoy it, too.

Thanks so much!

About the Authors

Stacy Claflin is a USA Today bestselling thriller author who has published more than 75 novels, including Girl in Trouble and The Perfect Death. She has always been curious about the human mind, and in her quest to learn more, she earned a degree in Psychology. Her favorite course was Abnormal Behavior, which has been useful in writing fiction.

Her love for thrillers goes back to her early childhood when she fell in love with Unsolved Mysteries and America's Most Wanted. When Stacy was five, she got mad at a babysitter who wouldn't let her watch the evening news. These days, she spends her free time listening to true crime podcasts or watching documentaries on the subject.

She has been telling stories for as long as she can remember, and as a child would often get into trouble for trying to convince friends her wild tales were true. Now she puts her creativity to better use by writing page-turning stories that leave readers begging for more.

Nolon King writes fast-paced psychological thrillers set in the glitzy world of entertainment's power players with a bold, insightful voice. He's not afraid to explore the darker side of human nature through stories featuring families torn apart by secrets and lies.

Nolon loves to write about big questions and moral

quandaries. How far would you go to cover up an honest mistake? Would you destroy your career to protect your family? How much of your soul would you sell to get the life of your dreams? Would you cheat on your husband to keep your children safe? Would you give in to a stalker's demands to save your marriage?

Also By Nolon King and Stacy Claflin

Dead For Good

Dead For Good

Left For Dead

Dead Of Night

Wake The Dead

Dead For Life

Once Upon A Crime

Once Upon A Crime

Twice Upon A Lie

Three Times a Murder

Stand Alone Novels

Lost and Found

A Simple Kill

Blown

Miserable Lies

Secrets We Keep

Close To Home

Heat To Obsession

Tell Me No Lies

Fade To Black